She'd baked him his own pie.

Carl felt so touched by that little gesture. True, the apples and flour and everything else had come from his grocery shopping. Still, that pie cooling on the countertop with a C cut in the top instead of regular chicken-track vent marks touched him. Maybe because no one else in Redwing would have thought of it.

No one else anyplace would have thought of it. Carl probably couldn't come up with the names of five human beings who truly cared about him. Only his dog, Four, hunkered in his corner, basking in the reflected warmth of the kitchen, would care. And now, perhaps, Grace and the children.

With each passing day, even each meal, she seemed more at home in his house. Little things he hadn't ever thought of cleaning had been scrubbed, polished, waxed or shined.

But she'd never indicated anything but gratitude for his kind treatment. Even if she'd baked him his own apple pie.

LYNN BULOCK

Lynn Bulock has been writing since fourth grade and still enjoys it as much as she did then. She's been married for over twenty years to her high school sweetheart. They live near St. Louis, Missouri, with their two sons.

Gifts of Grace
Lynn Bulock

Published by Steeple Hill Books™

STEEPLE HILL BOOKS

ISBN 0-373-87080-9

GIFTS OF GRACE

Copyright © 1999 by Lynn M. Bulock

Visit us at www.steeplehill.com

Printed in U.S.A.

I will repay you for the years the
locusts have eaten.

—Joel 2:25

To Joe, always

And

To "little Joe," "Triple J," "Bula"
and "Joey-Joe-Joe"
I love you all.

Prologue

"What am I going to do?"

Standing in her cold living room long before dawn, there were no people to keep Grace Mallory company and very little furniture to deaden the echo of her own voice. The battered couch had come with the rental house, although the afghan draped over it was hers, one of her few prized possessions. Feeling a chill, Grace picked up the coverlet and wrapped it around herself.

She needed a hug. She needed a lot more than just one hug, but the soft old coverlet's embrace was as close to that as she was going to get. "Aunt Jo, what am I going to do?" she mused to the woman who had raised her and crocheted the afghan. Grace had no idea where Jo was now, or where she had been for years. She might even be with the Lord she loved so much and had told Grace about so many times.

Wherever she was, Jo would have known what to do. Grace didn't know. She'd been so worried about the children. This was their third Christmas in a row without their father. First he'd been in jail, then last year before the holidays he was killed in an inmates' brawl. Now, her memory of him had faded, but the legacy of pain and poverty he'd left behind was still here: She had nothing to give the children for Christmas.

Her son Matthew had been concerned about that—not for himself, but for little Maria. At age ten, Matt was sure he was too old and tough for Christmas to matter. At bedtime last night he'd stood before her at the kitchen table. "Don't worry about Christmas. I took care of it," he'd told her. Grace had been too worried about other things at the time to give the matter much thought.

But at three this morning when she couldn't sleep, something had drawn her downstairs. The wrapped presents under the tree, even if they were few, filled her with dismay. Nobody would hire a ten-year-old to work in town, would they? Could Matthew have stolen these things, and the bright paper to wrap them in?

Grace felt so helpless. She'd done everything she could to try to raise the children right, to keep them from making any of the mistakes she and their father had made. Now her heart told her things were terribly, terribly wrong. "What do I do?" she whispered. "What do I do?" It had started out as a question for Jo, but by the time she voiced it out loud, it was a prayer.

It had been a long time since Grace had prayed. She still believed in God, but wasn't He just up there someplace watching? Surely He didn't care about her. That was pretty obvious in the downward spiral her life had taken in the last few years.

Wait. Watch. Pray. The words were as clear as if someone standing in the room with her had spoken them. Grace stepped back, stunned. Wait, watch and pray? She could do that. The wait-and-watch part, too. She looked out the window, where ancient drapes framed a frosty scene. Outside? Surely it was too cold to sit out on the porch and pray. And what if Maria called her? Grace was sure she was getting sick again.

Still, the porch drew her like a magnet. She went to the kitchen and grabbed a chair. Then, with the afghan still wrapped around her shoulders, she opened the front door and set the chair firmly on the front porch.

The chrome legs of the chair settled into a light dusting of snow. Grace smiled wryly. It really wasn't much colder on the porch than it had been in the living room. "All right, I'll wait. And watch. And pray," she said softly. Maybe God wasn't so far away after all. Grace couldn't help feeling that He was out there, someplace close by. For the first time in a very long while, hope poked into her heart, nudging aside the despair that was her constant companion. She settled in to wait the coming of the dawn, and whatever the day would bring.

Chapter One

Carl Brenner trudged through the snow, wondering why the house wasn't next door to the store. Not that it mattered most of the time. Most winters in Missouri didn't bring snow this deep before Christmas.

Today it was cold enough that he would have driven the pickup the five blocks between the house and the store. But that would have meant giving up one of the precious parking spaces in front of the store on the Redwing town square, and this time of year they were at a premium. So he and the yellow dog with no real name except Four—for his position in a line of yellow dogs that stretched back twenty-five years—walked in the bitter cold.

Right now, one of those moods had closed in on

him again—of wanting something. Except he didn't know what he wanted. He just knew it was out there, intangible and just beyond reach. No amount of prayer and Scripture had brought it closer, either. He was still running a store he didn't care much about in a town that didn't amount to spit. Granted, he never went hungry and he always had a roof over his head. He wasn't in debt. But he wouldn't miss anything in his life if anyone stole it, either. Except Four, and perhaps a pile of papers that would be meaningless to any other human being and didn't amount to enough physically to start a good fire.

The wind had died down once he turned the corner onto Main, where the buildings on the square gave some protection from the bitter breeze. Four perked up, and Carl looked ahead to see why.

The reason was quickly apparent and as quickly unwelcome. A delegation waited on the sidewalk, and it wasn't customers waiting for him to open the store. This was not the way to start the day.

Twenty minutes later the crowd had filed into the bank and Carl stood with them, shifting uncomfortably from foot to foot, dripping melted snow on the bank floor like everybody else. Like Four, mercifully curled up in a back corner so he wouldn't jump on people, Carl never felt comfortable during official town meetings such as this. He might have agreed to fill the empty seat on the town council, but he still didn't like these meetings.

"You know why we're here," Mayor Larry Trent finally began, looking at Carl. "It happened again yesterday. And I know he came in your place, too. This time you have to do something." The other two merchants nodded, Naomi from the café most emphatically.

Carl just couldn't stir up the same kind of righteous indignation as the rest of the group. "Now, look," Carl warned the shorter, portly man. "I have a store to run, and it's Christmas Eve. I don't see why I should be the one to go out to that farm and tell Grace Mallory she's raising a thief."

Mayor Larry Trent smiled uneasily. A squiff of his mouse-brown hair stood straight up, probably part of that patch he usually combed carefully over the bald spot at the top of his head. It gave him a comic air that belied the empty bank's frigid, formal atmosphere. "We can get somebody to watch the store for you, Carl," he coaxed. "Besides, it just doesn't look right, my going. The bank is the one place the kid doesn't ever take anything from."

"Wish I could say the same," huffed "Doc" Conrad, the town pharmacist. "I lose ten bucks every time that kid comes in the drugstore lately."

Carl huffed. The bank wasn't getting any warmer, and he had plenty to do next door before opening up. "Why don't we get you to do this? Or Ed? I mean, what are we paying him for as police chief, if not for stuff like this?"

"Because Doc would scare her to death. And if we let Ed in on this, it's going to get official," Naomi said, looking like the grandmother she was. "Then we're talking the county juvenile hall for a ten-year-old. He's a thief, but he's not even a good thief. Surely we can handle this ourselves and keep it quiet."

The anger rising in Carl nearly warmed him. "It's not like I'm taking home a lost dog, here. I'm going to have to tell the woman her kid's been stealing the town blind."

"And you'll do a fine job of it, Carl," intoned the mayor in his best professional voice, his plump white hands steepled in front of his white shirt. "Why don't you give me the key to the store?"

Carl trudged back home to get his truck, thinking very unchristian, un-Christmaslike thoughts about his mission. This time Four didn't stop anyplace along the way, just followed obediently, seemingly aware of his master's mood.

As he and Four got into his truck, Carl hoped he'd recognize the house, and the woman, once he got there. He knew the Mallory family rented the old Krieger place. It had gone to seed so badly after old Mr. Krieger lived there alone. Mrs. Mallory and the two kids had moved in about two years ago.

He tried to remember what Mrs. Mallory looked like, the times he'd seen her. Pale hair, he recalled. A pale, narrow face. Not very tall, and not very wide. Past that, she was a cipher. Carl had guessed that maybe she was afraid of him.

Of course, many people seemed intimidated by his size. Not that Carl enjoyed it much himself. At well over six feet, he was constantly hitting his head on things or having to fold himself up to fit somewhere, like in the overly narrow pews at church.

Carl could vaguely remember the younger Mallory child. He recalled it was a girl, but like her mother she remained a shadow in his mind. The family didn't go to the church in town, so his knowledge of them socially had been nil.

About the time he'd admitted to being hopelessly lost, due to the heavy snowfall the inkling of a path up ahead led away from the road. Carl turned the truck onto the poorly kept track, immediately sliding on the icy gravel beneath the deep snow.

At first the Mallory house was just an outline on the horizon, then it came into focus as a gray heap of lumber ahead. It looked awfully small—even for a family of three. Only the covering of snow smoothed out the uneven stubble of the fields. The barn roof sagged at one corner, and the shack that seemed to pass for a chicken coop looked as if a good wind would blow it over. A widow and two kids left on this rattletrap farm.

"What a Christmas!" Carl said aloud, expelling a tired breath. The dog leaned up against him, looking for warmth and comfort, and Carl had little of either to give.

Jake Krieger made a lousy landlord. Why hadn't he painted this place, and done more repairs? Surely he wasn't expecting a single woman as a tenant to do his work for him. Carl knew just enough about Grace to believe she would have fixed the place up if she had the money, but it wasn't her job.

It was coming closer. Grace hadn't really been aware of the truck until it slewed in the gravel as it turned off the main road. She shifted in the chair, marveling that day had already dawned. She had been so numb with grief that turned into anger and confusion that she'd been oblivious to it growing lighter.

Now it was Christmas Eve morning, and instead of the police car pulling in as she'd expected, someone else drove toward her through the snow in a black pickup. She pondered that in her mind, but no explanation came—probably because she was so cold and so tired and so entirely worn-out that no answers to anything were going to come right away.

She didn't recognize the driver even as the truck came closer. It wasn't Ed Dobbins, that much she knew. Relief warmed her stiff body. That meant that what she had been contemplating since before dawn—what she had been steeling herself for—she wouldn't have to do. Not now. Not today, anyway.

If Ed did come to the house, he was going to have to arrest her before he got Matt. That much she had decided in the predawn hours. By morning she'd wavered, picturing her children in separate foster homes if she went to jail. Would that be any better than just letting them take Matt?

She still couldn't figure out the identity of the man up ahead. He was tall sitting in the truck seat, and even as he got out there was a powerful depth to his body.

Someone sat beside him on the seat. Not someone, exactly, Grace saw, as a big yellow dog leapt out of the pickup behind the man.

As the two drew closer and came up to the fence line, Grace found herself more aware of her stiff, cold body. She wondered if she could rise from this chair.

The man was nearly at the porch now. This close she could see who it was, although she couldn't think of his name—the storekeeper from town, the one who always treated her like a real person when she was in his store. Why had they sent him instead of the police?

"Mrs. Mallory? Can I come up?" Carl asked as he stopped at the bottom of the steps. She was as he had remembered her and much more. Her pale hair was a yellow lighter than corn silk, pulled back severely to frame a face that looked much too narrow. Strands of it straggled out of the band that held them. The woman's eyes were dark and clouded like those of a wild animal, and there seemed to be smudges under them. She looked so fragile in her faded jeans that a good puff of wind would probably have knocked her down. This was going to be difficult.

"You're welcome. It's about Matt, isn't it?" She sounded tired. "You're not with the police. Does that mean he's not in trouble?"

The dog whined beside him, and Carl put down a hand to quell him. "No, ma'am, he's still in trouble. Could we go inside?" He started toward the porch steps which were still covered with new snow.

"If you're here to arrest him, I don't want to go inside," Grace Mallory said. Up close she didn't look as wild—just muddled. Looking at the quilt thrown over her faded jeans, though, Carl wondered if she'd spent the entire night in that chair. Her clothes had a frosty look to them.

For a moment he questioned her sanity.

"I don't have the authority to arrest him," Carl told her. "We can just consider this a warning." He went up the steps, which creaked under his weight.

Being on the porch made him more conscious of his size than ever. The roof hovered bare inches above his head, and he towered over the woman, which made him feel like a thug.

"So the things I found... Matt didn't buy them, did he? He doesn't have an after-school job in town."

His task refused to get any easier. "That isn't exactly what happened," Carl replied, shifting his weight uncomfortably. The wind didn't get to them here, but the cold sure did. How could the woman have spent the night here?

She looked up at him, the expression in her dark eyes more focused and alert. "What *is* going on?" she demanded sharply. "If you're not going to arrest him, what's going to happen now?"

Carl took a deep breath. "The boy's been stealing from every store in town—even Miss Naomi's Café. They sent me out here to tell you, and say that it has to stop." As he spoke, Grace Mallory stood straighter for a moment and then her eyes widened and she swayed. Carl readied himself for the female hysterics he expected to follow.

Instead, she came upright again and asked, calmly, "You're really *not* going to try and take

him away?'' Her eyes were even wider with surprise, and as innocent as those of his dog.

''Hadn't planned on it,'' Carl confirmed, ready
for the protestations of her son's innocence to begin.

''Then we'd better go in and talk to Matt,'' she
said. ''He's got an awful lot of explaining to do.''

Carl didn't know what took him more by surprise at that moment. At first it was her attitude—
totally the opposite of the defending mother he'd
expected—and then her actions that startled him.
As Grace Mallory turned to swing open the door
to the sagging house, the gravity of the situation
must have caught up with her, and she lost her
balance on the snowy porch. She was fainting or
falling—Carl couldn't tell which—and she was
headed for the ground if he didn't catch her first.

Chapter Two

Her body felt very cold and impossibly light, Carl thought, as he caught her. But even as light as she was, Grace Mallory filled his arms so that he couldn't reach the doorknob. He stood in front of the door, flummoxed, with his burden of woman and coverlet in his arms, and the dog whining and winding around his legs. Should he kick on the door and hope those kids were awake and would open up?

Before he could kick, Matthew opened the door. The boy's coltish arms and legs poked out of his shirt and jeans, and his pale hair looked even more disordered than his mother's. As soon as the door was all the way open, the boy's eyes widened as much as Grace's had and he launched himself at Carl. The dog barked at someone charging his master, but Carl called him back and he sat. The boy cried out, still launching himself at his much larger adversary.

"Mom! If you've hurt her..."

"I didn't hurt her. She fainted or something," Carl said, brushing past the boy as gently as he could. "Is there someplace to put her?" How could someone who couldn't be much more than five feet of skin and bones make his arms ache like this?

Matt still looked at him suspiciously. "In the living room." The Mallorys' "living room" was not made for living. It was as cold as the bank lobby and almost as empty. Carl was surprised that the scraggly Christmas tree wasn't decorated with icicles. "Maria. Move, now," the boy said with noticeable gentleness.

A small girl, with even more wild hair than anyone else in the family, slid off the beat-up couch that was the only piece of furniture in the room. As the child stood, she whimpered.

"She's sick," the boy said. "You sure Mom's going to be okay?"

"She'll come around in a minute," Carl said as he deposited his burden and started probing for a pulse in the woman's cool throat to see if he was right. Her even breathing reassured him, but the feverish feel of her skin under her shirt collar worried him.

She murmured something, and then her eyes came open. They were the same shade of brown as both her children's eyes, Carl noted, and they were as confused as a baby's. "What happened?" she asked.

"You passed out or something. Thought you needed to be inside," he explained. "Could you sit up and drink something warm?"

"I can sit up, I think." Her thin hand passed over her hair, all loosened now by Carl's clumsy efforts to get her inside the house. "I doubt there's something warm to drink."

"There's no milk," the boy said, sounding apologetic. "I wrapped Maria in another blanket. But she says she's hungry."

The little girl nodded, and made a noise somewhere between a sob and a mew. She moved toward her mother, flinging thin arms around her neck. She didn't move with a lot of energy. Carl puckered his brow as he looked at her. "The boy says she's sick?"

Grace's eyes clouded even more, then cleared and she stared down at her own lap, putting one arm protectively around the child. "Another ear infection, I suppose. I kept her home from school yesterday, hoping she'd be better."

"But you didn't call the doctor?"

"Don't have one. We go to the county health clinic when we can. I knew there wasn't money for medicine even if I went, so we didn't go,'' Grace said simply. Her outthrust chin dared him to say anything.

Carl lost his balance in surprise, and went from crouching beside the couch to sitting on the floor. The rug under him felt coarse and cold. ''No doctor at all?''

''None. I guess we could get vouchers or something if we went on welfare, but I'm not about to do that, Mr.—''

''Brenner, Carl Brenner. From the store in Redwing.''

''The store part I remembered, Mr. Brenner. Just your name escaped me.''

Her husky voice had a little bit of the South in it. The boy's voice when he spoke sounded sharper. ''Are you sure he didn't hurt you, Mom?''

''Not at all. In fact, Mr. Brenner caught me so I didn't fall out there. Mr. Brenner and his dog, I think. Where did he get to?''

''Still out on the porch. If I'm going to be here a while, could I call him in? He's clean and gentle. He'll stay in a corner.''

''Of course,'' Grace said. ''Not even a dog should be out too long in weather like this.'' She looked at Carl again, communicating much with few words. ''Are you sure about what you told me out there?''

''Yes, ma'am. I saw things myself.''

She sat up a little straighter and pushed her hair behind her. "Then could I ask you to give me a moment alone with my children? If you could put some water on for tea or something, to thaw us both out..."

Carl nodded. What little he'd seen of Grace Mallory so far told him that she could handle the difficult conversation with her son well—perhaps better if Carl left the room. He whistled Four in off the porch, and shut the door behind him. Going down the narrow hallway, they entered the only other door opening off it besides the living room, and Carl told the dog to lie down. Four found the most out-of-the-way corner and settled in.

The kitchen was a good size, but poorly furnished. There was a dinette set that looked far older than the children, the three chrome chairs around the table matching the one on the porch, and a small array of metal kitchen cabinets. The chipped countertops were clean but empty. There was no microwave, no coffee maker, not even a toaster oven. Judging from the limited range of kitchen appliances, it wasn't fancy cooking that went on here.

There was a battered teakettle on the stove, and he took it to the sink. The water still ran when he turned on the faucet, so at least the county was getting paid basic utilities. Either that, or the place had a well.

He filled the kettle and put it on the stove. The burner turned on with a whoosh when he turned the knob. This far out there would be a propane tank someplace in the backyard. Carl was willing to bet there was precious little in it.

While the water boiled Carl scavenged for tea or instant coffee, and thought about the boy's reaction to him bringing Mrs. Mallory in off the porch.

Carl knew that if his own mother had been alive when he was that age, he would have tried to take anybody apart who hurt her. He remembered what he'd done when he hadn't been much older and somebody had sicced a hunting dog on the original Yellow Dog.

There was scarcely any food in the kitchen. The more Carl looked around the place, the more his opinion of the young mother changed. He'd expected to come out here to find a woman who would deny her son was stealing and get in his face. Instead, a nagging thought was taking hold: Matthew Mallory was stealing to keep his family together, and hiding it from his mother.

This changed the complexion of things a bit. Carl shook his head. There had to be something he could fix for breakfast to go along with the tea. Looking around, he didn't find much. No dry cereal, only half a loaf of bread. Peanut butter in the pantry, and part of a box of oatmeal. Matt had been right; there was no milk except powdered. That would do mixed with water as liquid for oatmeal, Carl reasoned. He started reading the box.

Before he could get oatmeal on the stove, the boy came into the kitchen, backhanding the evidence of tears from his face. "Did you have to tell her?"

"Yeah, I did. You're big enough to know stealing is wrong. You're lucky it's me out here and not the police chief. If it was him, you'd be going to juvenile hall, or a foster home."

The boy tried to look tough. It didn't work very well. "Would you have given me a job if I asked for one?"

Carl stood beside him for a moment, feeling more awkward than usual. The boy looked up, his eyes bright. He seemed to sense Carl's discomfort. "You know I wouldn't. But there are alternatives." Carl put a hand on his shoulder, feeling the prominent bone under his fingers. "There's a whole town about six miles down the road, willing to help if you ask. You don't have to be a full-grown man at—what, eleven?"

"Ten." He said it looking down at the floor, as if ashamed to admit less age than Carl had guessed.

"Ten, then. It's an age to go to school and stay out of trouble. There will be ways for your family to get on. We'll see to it."

The boy's eyes held a challenge Carl could have

recognized in himself at the same age. "Yeah, well, it won't be welfare. Mom won't go for that. Or charity from some church, either. That's why we moved here in the first place. Some goofy church adopted us for Christmas when my dad was still alive and in jail. And they wanted to do it again last year once he was dead. Mom wouldn't have it." The boy seemed to run out of words. He looked up at Carl. "Do you play basketball?"

Carl had to laugh. "I'm not that tall. Only about six-three, maybe six-four."

Matt gave a low whistle. "That's still pretty tall. You wouldn't fit inside that henhouse out back."

"Would I want to?" Carl asked. "If there's chickens in there I could scramble eggs for breakfast instead of cooking oatmeal."

"No chickens. We would have eaten them if there were," Matt said with great practicality. "I mean, I'm pretty good, but I couldn't steal chicken feed."

Carl looked at him sharply. "You're not pretty good. You stink as a sneak thief. For which I am very thankful, because if you were good at it you would still be doing it."

"Hey, if I were good at it we'd be having Christmas," Matt challenged. "But I've got one up on you. You don't know how to make oatmeal, do you?"

Carl felt chagrined at being found out by a ten-year-old. "Not a clue. I cook the kind you dump in the microwave. Want to give me a hand, here?"

The boy's thin face split with the first grin Carl had seen from him. "I may stink as a thief, but I can cook oatmeal," he said. "Watch and learn."

The warmth of the kitchen felt welcoming. Carl noticed that the boy's worn sneakers looked awfully small for his tall frame, and narrow, as if perhaps they had belonged to someone else first. Carl was pretty sure he could see sock through a couple of holes.

The boy was at the stove stirring the oatmeal. Carl hoped he knew what he was doing. The kid had been impressed that Carl had thought of using the powdered milk to fortify the stuff. It looked less like wallpaper paste that way. He wished there was some cinnamon to go with the brown sugar in it. Or raisins. Some Christmas Eve breakfast this was for anybody.

Matthew tried to sound nonchalant as he stirred the oatmeal and talked at the same time. "A while ago when you were talking about foster homes? It sounded like you knew something about that."

"I do," Carl said. Nobody else in Redwing knew how much he knew about that particular subject. Redwing's knowledge of Carl began when he was a skinny, gangly young teen, come to live with his mother's brother, Jim. He struggled over how much to tell the boy. "I saw a few foster homes before I was your age. Trust me, you'd rather be here with your mom."

"Yeah, but wouldn't it be easier on her if I weren't?" The pain in the young boy's voice was agonizing for Carl.

"No!" he said sharply—more sharply than he'd intended. He noticed that Matt nearly dropped the spoon. "Take my word on it, your mom would rather have *three* of you getting into trouble all day long right under her nose than give you up." He'd only really met the woman this morning, but that much was evident.

He wished there had been someone to tell him that at age ten. Of course, by then he was an orphan in the third foster-care home he'd been in, with Yellow Dog the only constant in his life and childhood nothing but a vague, troubling memory. Even if someone had told him that, it would not have been the truth. But for Matthew it was, and it seemed to comfort him some. "That stuff ready to put in bowls yet?" Carl asked, trying to do the man-to-man thing and ignore the tears that threatened to engulf the kid again. Besides, he needed time to think himself. He was getting an idea. It was a crazy one, and it needed some working out. And it was the last thing he would have considered while driving out here. But suddenly this crazy idea sounded like exactly the right thing to do.

* * *

He cooked them breakfast. The wonder of it pushed through the confusion that clouded Grace's thoughts. This strange man, whom she barely knew had come to tell her that she could lose her son if she didn't find a way to get him to stop stealing from every store in town. And then, instead of nodding briefly and leaving her outside on the porch like any normal man, he had stayed around, and had picked her up when she'd fainted.

Since then, he'd done nothing but surprise her. His elegant movements and rough clothing were a contradiction of each other. The black pants and white shirt were certainly not the finest. He looked like someone who didn't care much about quality as long as his clothes fit, which she suspected was a challenge, given his tall, broad frame. His jacket hung oddly, as if he had the habit of shoving his hands and small heavy objects into the sagging pockets. His dark brown hair needed a trim. But despite all that, he looked as genteel as a prince in disguise.

And he cooked them breakfast—steaming tea, and oatmeal as good as anything she could have put together.

He sat at the table watching them eat. When she motioned toward the bowls with a questioning look at him, he shook his head. Grace itched to stroke his unruly, thick dark hair as she would little

Matt's. It looked as if it would be springy and alive under her fingers.

Wondering where that thought had come from, she stared down at her bowl in silence. It surprised her that she could eat. Surely everything she had been through lately should have rendered her incapable of eating. But she knew she had two children to raise, alone. It wasn't ever going to get any easier. Matt's disaster here had pointed that out. It was time to move on, take some action.

"Do you need any help in that store of yours in Redwing?"

The question seemed to startle Brenner, whose eyes widened. Grace couldn't tell if he thought she was being rude or just insensitive in front of the children. She hated to tell him that they'd dealt with much harsher realities already in their short lives than planning shoplifting restitution at the breakfast table.

"I don't hire kids. Especially ones not even in their teens." The man didn't seem to have a lot of spare words. That was all right. She wouldn't have known what to do with a talkative man. "Besides, how would any of you get there?"

Grace looked at him. "That junker outside runs. It doesn't look like much, but it does still run most of the time. It ran well enough to get me to and from work on the line at the paper plant in New Hope until I got laid off before Thanksgiving. I can hold a job. I'm capable.'' She seemed to have surprised Brenner by reading his thoughts. He looked embarrassed. ''Besides, getting there may be a lot shorter trip soon. This place is falling apart over our heads. If the landlord doesn't do something about it, I've told him I'm not signing a new lease next week. What is it, Mr. Brenner?''

''Just trying to figure things out. Right now it seems I came out here to solve one set of problems and got a different one instead.'' Carl looked around the room. ''No phone, right?''

Her nod confirmed what Grace was unwilling to say. She hadn't been able to afford a phone since they'd moved here.

''Still got a county phone book someplace?''

''It's down in the far right drawer,'' Grace said, watching Matt spring up to get it.

''Great. You know what a cellular phone looks like?'' Carl asked Matt.

Grace watched her son as he swallowed the last of his tea and nodded. ''Sure.''

''Good. Mine's on the seat of the truck. Go bring it back in.'' He handed the boy a set of keys.

Matt's eyes widened as big as the mugs they were drinking out of. Grace wondered what he'd say. Brenner was treating him almost like an equal—not a situation the boy was used to with any grown man.

Matt grabbed the keys and headed out the door.

"I can't remember all the numbers I need. We need to get Doc out here with some medicine. He'll make a delivery if we can get somebody from the clinic in New Hope to prescribe something. That child needs something today."

Grace couldn't have agreed with him more. And just now, she didn't relish being alone with the children. Even after hot tea and a little food she felt strange, as if she might float away if she didn't keep herself firmly tethered.

Matt came in with the phone and the keys. "All right," Carl said, looking up from the thin phone directory. "And you didn't even lock the keys in the truck. I do that about once a month, myself."

Matt grinned. "You're too big to fit through the window, too."

"You bet. I finally had Ed show me how to use one of those metal jimmy strips to get in. But I'm not gonna show you."

"Good," Grace said tartly. "We don't need to advance his illegal skills any."

Carl shrugged and dialed his phone. He made several calls—a little cryptic, when hearing only his end of the conversation. Finally he made another call, and during the conversation told the other person to hang on. "I need a pencil and paper," he told Matt.

He'd seen that Grace wasn't going to be able to get up and help, because Maria had fallen asleep on her lap. Matt nodded and quickly brought them. "Okay," Carl said into the phone, and listened for a while. Then he put the phone down again.

"If I drew a map to this place, could you ride into town with me and ride back with Doc to help him find the way here?" he asked, looking at the boy.

Matt looked at him, swallowing hard. "I think so."

"Good. Doc does a lot of things real well, but finding new places on unmarked county roads isn't one of them." He spoke into the phone a little more, then hung up. Matt settled down to watch Carl draw the map, putting in comments once in a while.

He even writes gracefully for such a big man, Grace thought. She was surprised that Carl could make an act look both masculine and graceful at the same time.

Matt seemed spellbound. While he leaned his elbows on the table to watch the proceedings, Grace shifted Maria a little and coaxed the fitful child to eat more.

She shook her head, pushing away her mother's hand. "Hurts. Don't want anything to eat."

"How will you get strong again if you don't eat, sugar?" her mother coaxed. But Maria wanted nothing more than a lap to cuddle in. Finally giving up, Grace settled the child in even more firmly and sipped the last of her warm tea.

Then she sat back in the chair, bone tired and almost oblivious to anything going on around her except her own thoughts. Because her husband had left her a penniless widow with no place to call her own, Matt had decided to solve that problem now by shoplifting. Grace thought that most women would be in a panic, faced with her situation.

Instead, it gave her the greatest surge of freedom she'd felt in a decade. For things to turn out this well when they had looked as awful as they had before dawn, God had to be watching out for them, after all. Those desperate prayers in the dark had reached someone Grace wasn't sure whether to believe in anymore. Perhaps they were all going to be all right, after all. As she sat wondering, the low, reassuring rumble of Carl Brenner's instructions to Matt lulled Grace to sleep in the warm kitchen.

Chapter Three

❧

Grace woke up with a start some time later. How had she and Maria both gotten onto the couch? She had a vague memory of having been half led, half carried there by Brenner. Maria, settled in alongside her, was sleeping and felt a little less feverish. They were both nestled under her Aunt Jo's granny-square afghan. Grace was touched that this strange man had tucked them in, even though it was a rather clumsy job, before he'd gone out to fetch medicine.

As Grace grew more alert she was able to figure out what had woken her. There were the sounds of car or truck doors slamming outside and heavy boots stamping off snow. In a moment Matthew opened the front door quietly. "Mom?" he called in softly. "I think she's still asleep," he said, apparently to someone with him.

"No, I'm not." Grace tried to keep her voice down. "But your sister is, so come in quietly."

"Okay." Matt passed the message on, and Grace could hear several pairs of heavy feet in the hall. One of them had to be Brenner's, because no one smaller could thump that loudly while trying to be quiet. She almost giggled, picturing the effort.

In a moment there were three men, all in stocking feet, in her living room. Grace had settled Maria into the nest of covers and got up from the couch. She missed the warmth immediately, feeling slightly dizzy and cold.

"Mrs. Mallory, I'm sure you've met Doc Conrad, who runs the pharmacy in town," Carl said, holding out a hand to the older gentleman of the two strangers with him.

"And my son Tom," the pharmacist said proudly. "First-year resident at Barnes-Jewish Hospital in St. Louis. He's home for Christmas and he can prescribe medicine now. We brought him on his first house call." A father's pride shone in Doc's blue eyes, and Grace looked from one man to the other, feeling helpless.

"You didn't have to do that. I'm so sorry they pulled you away from your break," she apologized.

The young man grinned. "No need to be sorry. Once I'm done training I plan to come down here and be a family-practice doc. I'll be doing this every day. This is kind of neat." He looked over to the couch. "Is that the patient? I hate to say it, ma'am, but you don't look so good yourself."

"My daughter's the patient. And normally I'd thank you to keep your opinions to yourself, but I don't feel any better than I look. Maybe after you get done examining Maria we can talk about me." Grace felt stunned. What was coming out of her mouth? A request for help? For herself? This was a terribly odd day. It had started oddly and it was just getting stranger all around.

It had taken this long to realize that beside the battered sofa, where she could have reached out and touched him from where she'd been lying, was the dog. When she looked at him, his tail thumped, but otherwise he didn't move from his stretched-out position, guarding Maria. "He wouldn't leave when we did," Carl said. "That's unusual for him, but he seems to have decided you and the girl need protecting." Grace liked the kinship she'd seen between the big beast and his owner. And obviously, neither of them planned to let anyone hurt Maria.

Brenner was a pretty resourceful man. Grace wondered if he was married. If he was, there was one fortunate woman in Redwing. He wore no ring, but then her Matt never had, either. They hadn't had money for one nearly twelve years ago. Not that he would have worn it even if they did, Grace reflected. Matt Mallory had never been the kind of man to be tied down with a golden band.

Doc Conrad looked at Grace. "Could you bring a straight chair in here for Tommy? It would be easier to examine the child sitting down, I think."

"I can do my own requests, Dad," the young man said good-naturedly.

"I know, son. After all, you're the doctor now." The older man stood still, hand frozen in a gesture. "I just thought of something awful."

His son looked concerned. "What's that, Dad?"

"You really *are* the doctor now. That means if there's going to be a Doc Conrad around here, it should be you. Folks are going to have to go back to calling me Kermit."

Carl laughed, and Tom Conrad laughed with him. "Oh, no. We can't let you do that. I can be 'Little Doc,' or 'Doc Tommy,' or something. I can't imagine you having to be Kermit again. Mom says you haven't answered to that since before pharmacy college."

"I haven't, either," the older man said. "But it just seems fit—"

"We'll work it out later. For right now I can still be Tommy, Dad. Especially from you. And I would appreciate that chair," Tom added, turning to Grace.

She stood in the doorway, watching the goings-on as if entranced. Did men really relate to each other this way? Fathers and sons like adults, with kindness and concern for each other? It was new to her. She nodded and got the chair.

Coming back to the room with it, she saw the dog was still guarding Maria. She prepared to touch the child's shoulder. Before she did, she stooped down, cupped the large, furry jowls of the animal in her hand. "It's all right," she told him, so he wouldn't think they were going to hurt his new charge.

She sat on the sofa and settled Maria in her lap. The girl still wasn't really awake. Slowly, with Grace coaxing her, she sat up and answered the doctor's questions about pain and how she felt. He opened a very new-looking medical bag, took out an instrument, and peered into her ears.

The whole situation touched Grace just as the morning's events had. The boy had to be in his middle twenties, not much younger than herself. He looked about fourteen. Well, maybe eighteen. But he seemed to know what he was doing, and finally he pushed back the straight chair and sat looking at her.

"You were right on target, Mrs. Mallory."

"Oh, please, call me Grace. It's bad enough these older guys are calling me Mrs. Mallory—"

"But from somebody who looks like he ought

to be eating Christmas cookies instead of writing prescriptions, it's a downright insult, isn't it?'' Tom Conrad finished for her. He had a nice grin. It was infectious enough that Maria giggled when he smiled.

''That wasn't what I meant,'' Grace spluttered, feeling flustered.

''Oh?'' Carl was smiling, too. ''I gather from what you said I get classified as one of the 'older guys.' Since when is thirty-one an older guy?''

''Since I can remember you coming over to watch me when I was in grade school,'' Tom Conrad retorted. ''You've got six years on me, old man.''

''Thanks. Thanks loads,'' Carl groused. ''If that's supposed to be my Christmas present...''

''Only one you'll get from me. Now let me get back to diagnosing this kid. I like the sound of that. My first independent diagnosis.''

''Thought you said her mother diagnosed her, Dr. Tommy,'' his father piped up from where he leaned against the wall, smiling.

''Well, yeah, there is that.'' The young man looked a little crestfallen. ''Is she allergic to any drugs?''

''None that I know of,'' Grace said. ''She doesn't usually take much unless she's real sick. I can't take off work and run to New Hope to the clinic unless she is really ill. Or at least I couldn't until Thanksgiving when I got laid off. Since then, I've had all the time in the world.''

"How about yourself? You allergic to any antibiotics? You look like you could use whatever Tom is giving Maria," Carl interjected.

Tom Conrad stood, looking more like the man in charge. "Actually, she probably doesn't. The virus that gave Maria the ear infection to begin with won't respond to antibiotics. And most adults don't react to cold viruses with otitis media.''

"Whatever," Carl said, smiling a little. Grace could tell he was tickled by Tom's gravity.

"Is this why I'm out here?" Doc piped up. "Not only to witness this auspicious occasion but to make my own house call, as well?''

"You got it, Dad. This prescription isn't going to have to travel far." Tom finished writing with a flourish and handed the slip to Grace, who handed it over to his father.

"You can't be a real doctor," Doc joked. "I can still read this." After laughter and back pounding worthy of Tom scoring a winning touchdown, Doc went out to the car and brought back a vial of liquid.

"Brought a couple of things just in case," he explained, handing the medicine over to Grace. "No charge for this one. It was worth the couple of bucks to see Tommy in action the first time. Merry Christmas.''

"Merry Christmas," she echoed, looking down at the bottle of pink liquid. Yes, it was a very strange day.

Kayla Trent. Of all the able-bodied people in town that Larry could get to mind the store all morning, he'd chosen his own daughter. Carl muttered under his breath outside, raising a cloud of steam with his words, so as to let out all of his frustration before he actually had to face Kayla. He was thankful the dog had stayed in the kitchen at home, sleeping as if worn-out from the morning's excursion. Four detested Kayla even more than he did himself. Probably because she always spoke in baby talk to him, and the dog considered himself too intelligent to put up with such nonsense.

She sat on a stool at the counter, one hand pillowing her vacant, peachy face, her other fingers tracing a pattern on the countertop before her. There were goods left on some of the shelves, so she hadn't given the whole place away.

The bell rang overhead when Carl strode through the doorway. "Oh, Mr. Brenner," Kayla said, looking up dreamily. "You're back. Do you want me to stay and help out? This is the first time all morning I've been alone for more than ten minutes."

"I'll bet," Carl muttered to himself. When anybody who still had merchandise on layaway heard that Kayla Trent was minding the store, they gathered like a flock of vultures.

"Any money in the till?" he asked, trying to sound nonchalant.

"Twenty-seven dollars," Kayla said proudly. "Mrs. Green said she still owed you five on that big doll for Hannah, and then Bill Parker came down to get something for his mother. He came by twice," she added with a giggle.

Bill was one of Kayla's more persistent boyfriends, though what anybody would want with the vacuous teenager was beyond Carl. "Didn't he get what he wanted the first time? I know I had plenty of things he could have gotten his mom for Christmas."

Her eyes got even bigger. "He wanted panty hose for her, and I didn't know which kind to sell him. He didn't know which kind his mother wanted."

"'Which kind'?" Carl felt out of his depth. Kayla had a way of doing that to him, speaking plain English so earnestly but in such a convoluted fashion that he got lost in the conversation.

"Sure. *Which kind.* I mean, there's control top, silk, sandalfoot, regular, and then there's the size thing...." she droned on.

"But you got it straightened out," Carl said,

willing himself not to shake his head. It was beginning to hurt.

"Sure did," Kayla said proudly, standing and brushing down the red-and-green baby-doll top she wore over a white long-sleeved T-shirt and jeans. She looked like a Christmas-tree angel, and probably had just as much sense in her blond head.

"Well, I'm glad. I appreciate your helping me out, Kayla. Anybody else come in?"

"Lots of people. I wrote them all down, just like Daddy told me to. He said I should keep a list of everybody who came in so I could tell you."

Carl could have ticked off most of the names without looking. The five people paying him on time for things in the back room. At least Mrs. Green had left him five dollars. The rest had strolled out with their merchandise without leaving a cent. And he would never be able to convince Kayla that she'd done anything wrong by giving them things before they paid them off. It wasn't even worth trying.

"You know, Kayla, I expect you need to get on home," he said, helping her with her coat. When she was almost to the door he spoke to her again, making her turn around. "You tell your dad you did a good job. In fact, tell him I said I think you're ready to help him out in his business. Maybe even work on the books for him some, or be a part-time teller after classes.'' Let Larry get a taste of his own medicine.

Kayla burbled with laughter as she walked out to the sidewalk and down the snowy street. Carl smiled grimly, picturing her father's florid face when she suggested helping out.

He took off his jacket and went to the back room. At least she'd gotten the heat running. Now, if there was only something to eat. He was starving.

Of course, he'd worked hard all morning. He'd driven back and forth from the farm to town more than he liked to think. At least Tom had pronounced Grace shaken, but basically healthy. ''Needs a lot more to eat,'' he'd added. ''And a lot less worry. I don't see how they'll keep that farm.''

''There's no way. But I've got an idea or two,'' Carl had told him. Tom hadn't asked any more questions, and Carl hadn't volunteered any more harebrained ideas.

Carl's growling stomach distracted him again. Cheese and crackers. Not much of a dinner, but close at hand while he kept busy at the store counter. On Christmas Eve he expected a constant stream of customers until he shut the doors in the early-winter darkness. Women still one little gift short for Christmas, and children with new money from Grandma all needed something. Farmers would stop by to buy the wife a little something for tomorrow, and he knew Bill Parker would be back at least once more.

When you're that young, hope springs eternal, Carl thought.

When you're older, hope doesn't spring much at all. Carl already knew that from his own experience, so it was no surprise that the day flew by and he never got anything else to eat. At five it was dark outside, and he was ready to lock up.

In the long run Kayla hadn't cost him all that much. Most of the folks that had slunk off with their merchandise could be gently persuaded to pay their balance by New Year's. Lottie Green likely wouldn't, but she'd owed less than ten on the doll, and Carl knew it would be her daughter Hannah's pride and joy.

He looked at the one left on the shelves in the dimly lit store. It had pale hair like Maria Mallory, and he could picture it cradled gingerly in her arms. He wondered if she'd ever had a doll.

They would be cold out there at the old Krieger place. Probably hungry and in the dark, too. Suddenly Carl's need to get home and change clothes, eat dinner and go to the carol service at church transformed into a desire to do something as foreign to him as walking into a wall at full speed.

He wanted to give things away. He wanted to go home and get the truck, then come back here and load the bench seat with bags of candy and a good sturdy wool blanket. Maybe some boots if he could figure out which size would fit the gangly boy. And he wanted to take it all to a lonely farmstead out in the snow where a woman waited—a woman who wouldn't appreciate what she would see as charity.

Even picturing her determination to refuse his gifts didn't stop Carl from putting his jacket back on and going out. He was sure that determination would be followed by disbelief. He'd seen it once today already, when Tom Conrad had absolutely refused payment for his services, just like his dad.

Grace Mallory didn't believe that anybody would do something for nothing. And with a determination even fiercer than hers, Carl Brenner suddenly wanted to prove to her that there were plenty of people in the world willing to help her. It was something he needed to do for reasons that went far beyond Grace Mallory. Reasons that had more to do with the kind of Christmases he'd had as a child, and what—or mainly who—hadn't been there.

Chapter Four

By seven, Grace wondered why she had wished for company. Grace knew that most folks would be at church now. Without a sick child, she might have gone herself, considering the events of the day. Of course, the walls would probably have fallen in on her, to quote one of Jo's sayings.

Surely sitting alone would have been preferable to entertaining a silent, out-of-place Jake Krieger and his young wife. She didn't know who felt most uncomfortable—her young landlord, or his child bride. He apparently didn't know what to say, and his companion was so hugely swollen with child that she couldn't sit still long enough to say anything.

It was odd to see Jake here, but not totally surprising. She *had* told him she wanted to discuss the lease in detail, and the condition of the house, before she signed anything. Leave it to the clueless young man to come tonight.

So far, all her attempts at conversation had failed miserably, and Grace sat stirring her instant coffee, trying not to ring the spoon like a chime against the chipped cup's rim. The Kriegers had the two that were whole.

When Grace heard the crunch of tires outside, she actually smiled. Someone else was coming. She hurried to the front door to see a man descending from a pickup at the gate, his arms laden with bundles.

It was Carl Brenner. Even though Grace wondered what on earth he was doing out here again, any other human company besides the silent pair would be a relief. "Mr. Brenner. This is a surprise. Please come in."

"No, I can't stay long," he said, faltering to a stop at the front door. "There were just a few things I thought of…for the kids.…"

"I've already got a little Christmas Eve company. Come in and join us," Grace said, trying to sound cheerful. Carl drew back.

"I wouldn't want to horn in on a party. Who else is here?" His expression told her that he was curious. Grace bristled. Who was he to decide how she managed her life?

"My landlord. And I wish you'd come in and

join us,'' Grace said, trying to sound as if she meant it. As he stamped snow off his boots, she couldn't keep her eyes on his troubled face. Something else even stranger caught her attention. ''Mr. Brenner? Your coat seems to be…moving.''

If there had been more light, Grace expected she would have seen him blushing. The oddest expression flitted across the big man's features. It was entrancing. ''Oh, well. That. Guess I'd better come in a minute.'' Without further explanation, he entered the narrow hallway and made his way into the parlor. ''Jake.'' He gave a curt nod, arms still full. ''Good seeing you. Give me a hand, here?''

Krieger leaped up, looking grateful for something to do. Grace realized that the young man wasn't unfriendly, just ill at ease. He probably had no idea what to do with himself inside his grandfather's old house, dealing with her. Given a job to do, he began talking.

As he helped Carl divest himself of various parcels, the younger man answered a volley of questions that Carl put to him. Although Grace hadn't gotten a whole sentence out of him in an hour, in the five minutes it took for Carl Brenner to get himself unwrapped, unwound and sorted out, she learned that the Kriegers might be having twins, and that as soon after the birth as possible, they would finally be going to Oklahoma with the rest of the family.

Brenner's coat came off and was put with the rest in a pile in the hallway. Then Grace could finally see what had been making the gyrations at his front. Out of his vest popped a tiny head, giving a loud caterwaul that rose over the volume of the men's conversation. "A kitten?" she cried, rising from her perch on the chair. "You brought us a kitten?"

The little animal fit into one of Carl's hands. He looked apologetic. "I started out with a doll. But then I wasn't sure if most girls really played with them anymore. I stopped in town to ask Mrs. Green about it, because she has a girl. She also had a cat with kittens, and when I saw them…" he faltered for a minute. Taking a deep breath, he went on. "When I was five my folks died in a fire. I went to foster care, and I didn't have anybody—except for a yellow pup nobody else wanted. He was the runt of the litter. Couldn't catch birds for anything, but he sure listened good."

"The one you have now?" Maria piped up from the corner. Grace didn't know when she'd come into the room. Usually silent in front of adults, she apparently couldn't resist the lure of the animal. She came closer to see the mewling bit of fur.

"No. That yellow dog was three dogs ago. Guess that made him the great-grandfather of the one I've got now." Carl had telescoped down closer to the floor so he didn't tower over the little girl.

In the shadow of the large man in front of her, Grace could see the five-year-old boy, left suddenly alone. It helped to understand parts of today; why the large, somewhat-aloof man seemed to be drawn to her children. He had been a lonely child himself, once. A lonely child comforted by a yellow dog.

She knew that Maria would love to have a kitten. Her daughter looked up at her in silent question. "You may keep her if you want." Judging from the speed with which Maria settled herself on the floor to make a lap for the tiny animal, she wanted her. Grace watched Carl as he put the kitten in Maria's lap. Her daughter's fingers touched the orange fur, and the little creature quieted down and started curling up for a nap. Removed of his burden, Carl looked a bit awkward again as he straightened. "I brought kitten food, the dry kind. And the kind of litter Lottie's been using for them. It's all she'll need for a little while, that and water."

Grace was touched that he'd thought of everything.

"Would you like a cup of coffee?" she asked. "You must be near frozen, making that trip again, Mr. Brenner."

"I'd take one," he said solemnly, still looking down at Maria and her new friend.

Missy Krieger rose awkwardly from her place on the chair.

"Let me go with you to help make it," she said. Grace was about to refuse her offer of help when she thought of all the time she'd spent, at the end of each pregnancy, just walking around in circles because no other position felt just right. Instead of turning the young woman down, she nodded, and motioned her along the hallway into the kitchen.

Suddenly everything seemed lighter. So she only had eight dollars left from her unemployment check in the whole house, Grace told herself on the way to the kitchen. So they'd had pancakes for supper. Given the prospect of Maria having a real Christmas present of a tiny orange kitten, suddenly tomorrow seemed like a future.

Carl squirmed uncomfortably on the low couch, wondering if Grace had really heard Jake's words. She seemed oblivious to the young man's plans to be with the rest of his family.

Surely she would figure out any minute that she was either going to have to buy the place from Krieger or move. Soon. And from what he'd seen already, Carl knew that Grace Mallory didn't have the kind of money needed to buy this farm. She probably didn't have enough money to buy next week's groceries.

She sat across the room in the rocker and seemed a thousand miles away. She looked less wan than she had this morning, Carl thought. Her hair was once more pinned up into a tidy mass, still scraped back tighter than he would have liked to see it. More of it around her face would have called less attention to the sharp planes and dark hollows there. She was wearing clean jeans and a cream-colored sweater.

Carl found himself wondering what she'd look like in a dress, with her hair arranged in some sort of curls. Grace in a dress? He shook his head, wondering where that little bit of woolgathering had come from.

Fortunately, no one noticed. Krieger still kept on about Oklahoma, with his young wife listening raptly and nodding. Grace's attention had strayed from the young couple to Maria, who sat on the floor about five feet away and crooned to the kitten.

Carl was so glad he'd gotten it. The kitten was worth the trade he'd made with Mrs. Green to settle her debt. Now there were two happy little girls tonight, both with their heart's desire. Not that he would have thought of either of them on his own. Seeing Maria earlier in the day had made him decide that he would go back and give Lottie Gruber the doll for her daughter, but Kayla had beaten him to that. And the woman's gratitude when he'd come to her door in the dark and only wanted to know what she thought a six-year-old girl would want for Christmas had been amazing. She'd been more than happy to part with one of the kittens tumbling on the floor.

Seeing Maria with the kitten brought back so many memories, few of them happy. How many hours had he spent curled up on some narrow mattress with Yellow Dog? Whenever the unfriendly world had threatened to swamp him, the pup had always been there. He'd helped him carry the burdens no little boy of six or seven should have borne; the ugly stares and even uglier whispers of adults who'd never realized he'd heard what they said about his parents.

Animals truly made the best companions, he thought. His dog never reproached him for anything. He was always glad of a kind word and a few scraps. And those liquid brown eyes always understood, no matter what Carl had to say to him.

Why did some cats get so silly and contented when you laid them on their backs? Carl had never wondered about it before. Now, as he became lost in thought, oblivious to what Jake was saying. Watching the little orange puffball seem to smile up at the child made odd sensations crawl through the aching muscles of his chest and arms, tired from the exertion of the day.

The crawling sensations were only partly due to muscle fatigue. Partly, too, they came from looking around the room. It was so empty. Carl knew that the couch and the dinette set in the kitchen had belonged to Jack's grandpa. Nobody had wanted them when the old man had died, so they'd just stayed in the house.

The Christmas tree was tiny, artificial and pathetic. Again, he felt overwhelmed by unfamiliar feelings. These children—the girl on the floor, the boy standing stiffly by his mother's rocker—shouldn't have to sleep in this place tonight. It repelled him to think about them waking up on Christmas morning in the cold of the sparsely furnished rented house for another in what promised to be a series of bleak Christmases. He couldn't let that happen.

Jake had apparently gotten around to breaking the news to Grace while Carl had been watching the children. Because now Grace sputtered a little, quietly, looking hard at her young landlord. "I don't know, Mr. Krieger," Carl could hear her saying. "I know I can't buy the place. That's just out of the question. But I'll need a little time to figure out what I'm going to do next."

"You don't need any time at all," Carl heard himself say. "You can move into my place. I live alone and need help running the store. And there's an apartment in the back of my house, just five blocks from the store in town. We can pack you up tonight if you want.''

The room was so still after Brenner's pronouncement that Grace could hear the kettle hissing on the stove in the kitchen. Young Missy Krieger just sat on the hard kitchen chair with her mouth gaping open. Jake fidgeted uncomfortably at one end of the couch, just as silent.

The children didn't even seem to move, as Brenner leaned forward, seeming to wait for an answer. Without thought, Grace knew what her answer should be. Of course she couldn't do that. It would be charity. Scandalous charity, at that.

Her thoughts must have shown in her expression, because Carl was shaking his head, seeming to read her doubts. ''There's two rooms on the top floor of the house that don't open onto anything else. They have their own bath, and private stairs down to the kitchen. The folks that built the house originally had money. Planned to have servants all the time, I guess, because the house is built for it.

''Besides, if I want to get down to brass tacks, you owe me money. I figured working in the store could be the way to pay things off, and if you live that close, I know you'll get to work.''

Grace wanted to snap her refusal, and quickly. Then she felt the pressure of little Matt's hand on her shoulder. Its strength surprised her. She looked up into the thin face that had looked so young when she'd confronted him this morning.

Since then, he'd been so quiet. He shouldn't be worrying about what they were going to do next, Grace decided. And if she stayed on this farm, he would worry. If they stayed here she wouldn't have the resources to make his dreams come true. And if they stayed here, those dreams couldn't amount to much in the first place.

The man waiting for an answer didn't seem to know just how blunt his statements had sounded. Grace studied the odd figure who'd changed from stranger to protector in the course of one day. He wouldn't be easy to work for—of that she was certain. But he'd be fair and honest. And she knew instinctively that working for him would provide her with a better life than she'd had in a while.

It beat welfare. And she did owe Brenner money for things Matt had stolen. If she was frugal, she could be shed of that debt in less than a month by keeping house for him and helping at the store, even if she worked for minimum wage. Then maybe she could find another place in town and get on with some kind of life—a life that would let her feed and clothe her children, give them a decent home.

She could hardly wait to see the surprise in Carl Brenner's face when she didn't argue with his offer. He seemed every bit as stubborn and proud as Grace knew she was herself. But something was urging her to say yes to this. It felt like the same something—or someone—that had told her to wait and watch before dawn. Was this what she had been waiting and watching for? A strange man to walk into her life and offer to help her out with everything, when he should have arrested her son instead? It was so bizarre that Grace considered it.

She cleared her throat. "Mr. Brenner, I'll take you up on that," she said, waiting for the shock and amazement to cross his face. Of all the aggravating things, why did the man have to smile instead? She needed help in figuring this man out.

Chapter Five

❧

"Like a herd of turtles in a snowstorm!" Grace's pronouncement had the children laughing and Carl regarding her with a questioning look. He might have wondered if she was a little off-kilter before. Now Grace suspected he was certain of the fact.

Shrugging her shoulders, she turned to Carl again. "That's what my aunt always said when we started a trip. She was my great-aunt, really, and she raised me. She had this ancient station wagon the whole time I lived with her, and it always seemed it took us forever to get loaded up and go anywhere. Not that we ever went much of any-place. But even a trip to the store seemed to be a major endeavor."

It *had* been a major endeavor. Aunt Jo had always had to find something—her wallet or keys, and then a scarf or ball cap that covered her masses of red hair to her satisfaction. Then there was the station wagon—huge, blue and named Alice—which was balky at best. By the time all that was done, the day had always been half over. On good days they had moved as slowly as turtles in a snowstorm.

"We aren't moving much faster," Carl groused as if he'd heard her thoughts. There had been the children's things to pack up, and the tasks of somehow corralling the kitten and settling Maria in with the bags, bundles and a pile of quilts around her and her new Christmas present. The second seat in the pickup wasn't designed to hold so much, but somehow they made it all fit.

Grace felt like singing Christmas carols now. The landscape zipped by, covered in snow. Thinking about Aunt Jo made her remember the good Christmases of her childhood. Maybe this Christmas would be the start of a new beginning for them.

Carl's home, when she saw it, looked impressive. Even in the dark she could make out a high gabled roof with two broad stories and an attic, as well. The house gleamed in the faint moonlight with a fresh coat of paint. Somehow she could picture him in the cooler autumn days, up there with a paintbrush.

Shaking herself out of her goofy daydream, Grace opened the door and jumped down from the truck. The dog bounded out of the house through a large dog door and ran through the snow until he sat down in front of her, barking once. The noise accomplished what stopping had not, and woke the children in the back seat. "We're here," Grace said, watching Maria's head loll sleepily back onto the quilts piled beside her. "Help me get her down, Matt."

The boy nodded, backhanding sleep out of his eyes and standing in the narrow space between the seats. "C'mon now, Maria. Wake up so Mama can help you down." His sister murmured in her sleep, then sat up slowly and put her arms out to be carried in. She looked dazed and tired. "It will be all right, sugar," Grace told her. "We'll get you inside where it's warm, and in a bed soon. Just help me out, here."

"I'll take her," said Carl beside her, his voice gruff and firm. He leaned into the truck and picked up the child as if she weighed no more than the coverlet around her, and strode up the steps to the house. Somehow he found a way to open the back door and turn on the porch light. The kitchen was still somewhat dark, with only a light over the stove providing a faint glow.

Carl crossed the kitchen and stopped at a closed door. "The apartment. Can you open this for me?"

Grace was right behind him. "Sure." The old-fashioned key turned smoothly in the lock, and the dull brass knob felt cold and heavy in her hand. Opening the door brought cool air smelling of cedar.

"These stairs are a little narrow," Carl said, not turning around as he mounted the flight leading from the kitchen. "But we should be able to get anything you need up or down them."

Naturally the dog had to follow them. They moved slowly. The big dog lumbered up the steps, keeping even with Grace. "He really doesn't have a name?" Grace questioned Carl, stroking the dog's head.

"Just Four." He said it as if it wasn't unusual.

"That's unfair," Grace said.

Carl blew out breath in a puff that was almost a snort. "Unfair to who? I don't mind calling him Four, and he answers to it. Why call him something stupid, like Lord Randall's Conniption or something? He's just an old yellow dog."

"Still, everything ought to have a name."

"He's got enough name to suit both of us," Carl replied, finding a light switch with his elbow. A bulb in an older-looking ceiling fixture illuminated the square room.

"I'm sure it needs cleaning and airing. And the beds aren't made properly," he said, sounding apologetic.

"I got the impression you hired me as the house-keeper as well as working in the store," Grace reminded him. "You're not supposed to have a room ready like in a hotel." What she could see of the room in the dim light impressed her. There was more space here than in the bedrooms of the Krieger farmhouse, and the furniture was in better shape. The plain iron bedstead would be plenty big enough for her and Maria to share. "Is there a trundle someplace I could make up for little Matt?"

"Even better." Carl laid his burden of child and quilt down on the bed. "There's a second room next door. It isn't very big, but it will be good for the boy."

Matt came up behind them, with a bag and the protesting kitten. "My own room?" Matt sounded almost suspicious.

"Not much of a room. There's a bed and a dresser. Nothing fancy," Carl said. He didn't tell the boy it was a small, cramped room. If the boy was as happy with the narrow space under the eaves as he remembered being when it had first been his, he didn't plan to shatter his illusions.

"Come down and help me get your mom's things out of the truck." Matt didn't need asking twice to go back down the stairs. Carl turned to Grace. "There's bedding in that chest over there, I expect. I haven't been up here for a while. If it's not all right to use, tell me and I'll get you some from my side of the house.''

''All right,'' Grace said. She waited for him to turn on more lights. ''You're going to go down those stairs in the dark?''

''Done it plenty of times. Besides, if I turn on more lights, won't it wake up the girl?''

''It might. It's kind of you to think of it,'' Grace said. Listening to him go down the stairs, she crossed to the chest and opened it. The sheets folded on top of the pile of linens smelled sweet, like the cedar lining the chest. They would make a welcoming bed.

Rolling Maria gently from side to side several times, she made the bed without lifting the child out of it. The kitten was more of a challenge, being entranced by all the covers moving up and down. Grace had to fish her out of the wrong side of the sheets and quilts three times before she smoothed the last one down and settled the child—still in jeans and a shirt—under the covers, the kitten on top.

While Carl and Matt were still downstairs, Grace made Matt's bed. As she put sheets on the narrow bed, she could look out the equally narrow window of the small room. Outside she saw a light bobbing between a garage and the house, evidence that they were still moving things into the house.

Back in the main room, Grace sat down on the

closed chest and began to get ready for bed. Maria could sleep in her clothes tonight, but she intended to start her new life by putting on a proper nightgown before slipping between the sheets in her new bed. Her muscles protested as she untied her shoes and put them beside the chest.

By the time she'd found her nightgown and laid it out, Matt had stumbled up the stairs, the long day having finally taken its toll. He looked like a little boy again in the soft light. "Turn out that light on your way in, and go to bed. There's enough moonlight for me," she told him, as he went into the small room. She waited to see his light go out under the heavy oak door, and hear his steady breathing before settling down for the night.

For the first time in almost twelve years, there was no litany of her faults and mistakes of the day as her bedtime lullaby. That had been one ritual her pitiful lack of self-esteem had been happy to take over from Matt once he'd gone to prison that final time. What should have been a peaceful, pleasant time of day had always been instead a time for recriminations.

In all the blessed silence, Grace even wondered if she could hear sleigh bells and reindeer hooves. Certainly this peace, just beginning, was a gift from someone.

* * *

"What's the matter? Don't you know where you are?" Carl asked, trying to be as gentle as possible. The moonlight filtering through the window illuminated Maria's pale face and hair. Carl felt absolutely helpless. What did he know about little kids—crying or otherwise? Not enough.

Though unable to settle down, Carl had stayed in bed until Four had lifted his head and whined. He never did that at night unless something aggravated him. Usually it meant there was an animal out in the yard. As they'd padded down the stairs, though, the dog had headed toward the front of the house—not his usual post for spotting raccoons and rabbits. Still, Carl followed him and found the little girl in the parlor, her clothes disordered as if slept in, and crying softly.

"He won't know where to go," she said, making the last word nearly a wail. "I can't get my sock off. And even if I got it off, he won't know it's mine."

None of this made any sense to Carl. It seemed he'd spent the entire day at sea, listening to females, and that he was destined to spend the night the same way. None of them, no matter what size, had made perfect sense today. First Grace, then Kayla, and now tiny Maria—none of them spoke the same language he did.

"You don't want your socks off, Maria. Your

feet will get too cold up there in bed. Now, how about going back there, all right?''

His touch on her shoulder, which he'd wanted to be comforting and reassuring, was instead the last straw. The wailing began afresh, louder. ''No, I can't! If I go back now, he won't know I'm here. Or Matt. He won't come!''

''Who won't come?'' Carl asked her, beginning to have the faintest idea.

''Santa. Santa Claus won't come if he doesn't know where I am. Even if I put up my sock.''

Relief washed over Carl so strongly that he had to sit down on the floor to control his shaking legs. ''Santa Claus? Is that all you're worried about? Of course he'll come. And I guess we *will* need your socks. Both of them, won't we? Because Matt didn't hang one up, either, did he?''

She shook her head, done with her crying now that Carl understood. ''Will you help?''

She looked up with such trust. Carl had never undressed a kid in his life, and he hadn't intended to start tonight. But somehow the two of them found a way to get her socks off and affixed to the mantel. When they finished, he pointed the sleepy child back up the stairs to her room.

Carl wandered into the kitchen then, trying to remember where he'd put the unopened bag he'd brought to Grace's house. He had hard candy in a sack, and plenty of silly little toys for the boy.

Surely he could come up with something for Maria, as well. As he stood in the kitchen thinking, soft thumps cascaded down the stairs. The kitten stood in front of him, meaning to be let out.

He scooped up the tiny beast with its prickly little claws and deposited it just outside the kitchen door in the dishpan of sand he usually used to keep the porch free of ice.

"That will do for tonight. In the morning we'll get that box set up. You're an indoor cat." Carl shook his head. He was talking to a cat. It might be the first time, but Carl was sure it wouldn't be the last. In a moment he brought the cat inside the house and went in to fill stockings.

Carl knew that he made a decidedly untraditional Santa Claus—in bare feet, a sleeveless undershirt and rumpled black pants, and followed not by eight tiny reindeer, but by a huge yellow dog and a feisty orange kitten.

"He did come! He did! Mr. Carl was right!" Maria's incredibly shrill voice pierced the pale light of the room. Grace took in her words slowly.

"Who came, baby?" she asked, not believing what Maria had said.

"Santa. We put my socks out, one for me and one for Matt. And they're full. I can tell. Hurry, Mama. I want to go see again."

"All right. Let me dress first, and you get your brother up. We'll go down in a while."

Maria fairly bounced—a sign that the antibiotic must be starting to work. Grace could hear Matt protesting in the next room, and thanked her lucky stars that he wasn't the kind of big brother to tell Maria the truth about her stocking, even when rudely awakened.

Grace rose and stretched. The air didn't feel any colder than it had been in the farmhouse. She couldn't quite bring herself to think of that ramshackle building as "home," even though they'd lived there for almost two years. It was supposed to have been a stopgap, a place to stay until they got on their feet again. The trouble was, they never had.

But still she had to raise these children and keep them out of harm's way. Carl Brenner's attic seemed as good a place to do that as any.

She didn't spend too much time getting dressed, with Maria sitting impatiently on the edge of the bed, urging her to be faster. She'd even infected Matt with her excitement, and he stood at the door of his room, whistling.

Finally Grace was ready except for the heavy shoes it seemed she had taken off only moments before, to go to bed. She made a decision to leave them next to the chest. She wished for delicate, ladylike slippers to wear instead, but she was going to have to make do with her heavy white socks. If she sat down quickly in the parlor, perhaps no one would notice.

"Where's my kitty?" Maria asked, pausing in her jumping for a moment.

"I don't know. Maybe downstairs seeing what Santa brought. Let's go see, shall we?" Grace still couldn't believe that Carl had filled stockings for her children. She intended to pay him back for whatever she found in them, even if it meant working an extra week or two for him.

Once she got down to the kitchen, though, she began to doubt how much she'd be doing. Even this early, Brenner had obviously gotten up before her. A coffee maker bubbled on the countertop, and there seemed to be something in the oven. For someone who claimed to need a housekeeper, he seemed awfully self-sufficient.

In the parlor, a floor vent blew toasty warm air. Grace looked around the room and then back at Matt, who stood wide-eyed near the mantel, looking at the bulging socks. "Please go up the front stairs and knock on Mr. Brenner's door. Ask him if he would like to come down."

Matt gave the makeshift Christmas stockings one more look, then nodded and pulled himself away. He bounded up the stairs, then the dog barked as Matt knocked on the door. She could hear a hurried conversation between Matt's high voice and a lower one, then he came back down. "He's almost ready. He asked if we would wait."

"Of course." Grace had to keep reminding herself that she had agreed to be the hired help here, not a guest. She ought to see what she could do about breakfast, she thought to herself, heading for the kitchen.

The pan in the oven appeared to contain biscuits. They were the kind that came out of a tube, but there were plenty of them. Grace poked around in the refrigerator to find butter and jelly to go with them. In a day or two, she told herself, she'd know her way around this new kitchen and things would be easier.

As she looked in the cabinets for dishes, Carl came into the room. His hair slicked down with fresh combing and water, he wore a clean blue shirt. "Good morning. I think we're wanted in the other room. You are, at least," he said, dark eyes solemn. "Do you mind if I come, too?"

"It's your house, Mr. Brenner," she reminded him. "You are certainly welcome to do as you like. And I suspect there would be precious little to do if you hadn't gotten up in the middle of the night. I hadn't intended—"

"I know. I figured you hadn't, but those kids shouldn't do without Christmas because of what's happened. If anything, they need it more than ever."

Grace nodded, unable to speak. In the large and serious man before her she saw again the shadow of that boy he'd talked about last night. That boy who knew what her children were going through, and worse. Hadn't he lost both his parents? In that moment Grace wondered what anyone had gotten *him* for Christmas—then or now—or if anyone had even bothered.

She followed him into the parlor and sat on a very nice sofa, which felt as if it had never been sat upon often, given its age. Clearly, Carl didn't do much entertaining.

She only had time to sit before the children began digging things out of their stockings. "Candy…a ball…a yo-yo. Cool!" Matt sounded nearly beside himself. There were oranges in the toes and a handful of nuts. One object looked out of place in Maria's until Grace realized that the small ball of yarn was for the kitten, reminding her daughter of the present that didn't fit in her stocking.

Through all the mayhem the yellow dog sat in the doorway to the parlor, tail thumping. "All right," Carl said after the gifts were all admired, looking at the dog. It seemed to be his signal to enter the room, which he did with as much enthusiasm as the children had earlier.

Maria submitted with good humor to having her

face washed by the animal, then turned to look at Carl. "Where's his presents?"

"He doesn't wear socks," Carl said without smiling. Maria seemed to take his explanation at face value. Grace could see under the solemnity a side of Carl Brenner that she hadn't seen before, and wondered in fact how many people ever got to see it. He was actually teasing the child in a friendly sort of way. She could see a glint in his eyes, and he seemed just a flash away from grinning. He was enjoying watching them with their gifts.

And he must have felt her observing him, because he looked across the room at her then. Half a smile lifted one corner of his expressive mouth before he stood. "Can I help put breakfast on?"

"No, indeed. That's the kind of thing you hired me for." Grace got up and started to move briskly.

"Well, the dog needs out, anyway. I'll follow you to the kitchen."

Four's ears pricked up when he figured they were talking about him, and he followed them into the back of the house where full sunlight shone through the windows. "I hope you don't mind. My doing that and all," Carl said. He seemed like a boy again as he apologized, looking out the door after the dog instead of at Grace.

"Not at all, Mr. Brenner. I hope that you'll give me a bill later—for all the things you put in Maria's socks. We'll add that to my debt.'' Grace tried to sound as businesslike as possible while she set the table.

Carl closed the door firmly, almost slamming it. ''I'll do no such thing. Besides, Santa Claus filled those socks. You don't pay back Santa Claus, do you?''

''Not usually,'' Grace admitted. ''What's Santa Claus's favorite kind of pie? Perhaps we could find a way to have one for Christmas dinner.''

''Santa Claus eats any kind of pie on the planet. And today, Santa Claus could probably eat a whole pie by himself,'' the tall man said as he turned and left the room. This time Grace knew it was no illusion. This time he smiled as broadly as little Matt.

Chapter Six

Carl remained smiling most of the day, which mystified Grace. He definitely smiled through dinner, which he insisted they share at his large dining-room table. Grace could tell the formal dining room didn't get used much. She had to dust the table before laying it with a cloth and plates. His full kitchen was a joy to work in, and Carl seemed impressed when she brought out ham, mashed potatoes, a green-bean casserole and an apple pie.

The children were more than impressed. Grace had to give them several "mother looks" across the table to keep them from falling on the food like wolf cubs. It surprised her to see how resilient they were. Sort of like young wolves in that respect, too, she reflected. But then, healthy children in a better place than they'd ever been before were likely to eat.

After dinner, she went to Carl to talk about the hard things. "We have to go back to the farm. I need to get my car, pack up what little we've still got there."

"I figured you would. Do you want me to stay after I drive you out?"

"It's not much of a way to spend Christmas," Grace replied. "I probably already made you miss church."

Carl shrugged. "They won't miss me much. I didn't even think to ask if you wanted to go someplace."

"Nobody's going to miss me anywhere around here," Grace said. "I haven't been inside a church in years."

"Would you like to change that?" Carl asked softly. "I don't expect you to just follow along where I go, but it would be nice."

"I understand," Grace said, admiring his caution. She still wasn't used to a man who thought things through instead of just lashing out. One who actually asked her opinion seemed too good to be true.

"If you want to talk to the pastor, we could stop in for a minute on our way out to the farm."

"I hate to bother him on Christmas," Grace

said. It seemed rude to interrupt someone's holiday.

"He won't mind. He's got four kids, and they've all probably had so much Christmas by now that he's ready for any diversion."

Grace shook her head. "No, really. I couldn't bother anybody on Christmas. I will go meet him. Soon, all right?"

"Fine." Carl stood and stretched, again reminding Grace just how large a man he was. He could have been terribly threatening, and she wondered again why she'd agreed to work in his house with no company but two small children and a dog.

Still, size wasn't everything. Matt hadn't been much bigger than she was, but he'd constantly reminded her how weak, how defenseless, and primarily, how stupid she would always be, compared to him. Carl didn't seem to use his advantages in the same way.

"You want to change clothes or anything?" he asked.

"Just to get my jacket and make sure Maria takes her medicine before we go."

He nodded. "She seems better today."

"I think so. She'd only tell me if it was awful," Grace admitted. "She's a quiet one."

"I can relate to that. It's easier somehow if you are when you're a kid. People don't notice you as much." As he strode away to get ready to go,

Grace felt a shiver pass through her. How much of this man's childhood had been spent like that of her children, hoping that no one noticed him? Again she felt the need to reach out to him.

But she instinctively knew the protective layers around that inner child were too thick. Too much man covered up that child, and Grace knew that if she reached out to him she would be too aware of the large man before her to remember the inner child that needed the attention.

The truck took a while to warm up. Grace reflected in the silent interior that she still didn't even know what color Carl Brenner's eyes were, much less the more important things about the man who was now her employer. The few long looks she'd had at his face had revealed plenty, but never the color of his eyes.

She'd seen his concern for her children, and his delight over a warm apple pie. There had been affection for the animals, even the goofy new kitten. But were the eyes that showed all that blue or gray? Some color in between, as fluid as the man himself, Grace decided as they drove off.

When they got to the farm, the place looked shabby to her. She hadn't left it much except to go to work. So she didn't often look at it the way a stranger would. A stranger wouldn't think much of this place. Everything needed paint, and a missing shutter made a gap at one of the upstairs windows. All in all, it looked like a place that belonged to someone who didn't care about it.

Which Grace had to admit, was true. It had been a refuge, a cave, just someplace to hide out and put her life back together again after her marriage and widowhood. She'd moved there because the job in New Hope looked like a fresh start. Raising her kids in the kind of neighborhood she could afford in a bigger city wasn't an option.

The Krieger farm had been the closest available rental to New Hope when she was looking. It wasn't a long drive to the prison where Matt was still alive at the time. She had planned to visit him there, but he wouldn't have her or his children anywhere near the place. That was the only manly decision he had made in over eight years of marriage.

It was still hard to admit that marriage to Matt Mallory had been more difficult than losing him. If she'd known more about what to do, maybe she could have helped him more, Grace told herself. Maybe then, he wouldn't have sunk into his silences that went on for days, broken only when he found more liquor and slunk off to get drunk, after which he'd come back with plenty to say—none of it ever good.

At least most of it had been directed at her. As an adult, she could handle his foul moods and ugly temper. He'd always left the children alone, and Grace had told herself that someday it would all get better.

Except it never would have. She knew now that nothing better had ever been in store for Matthew Mallory. He'd died while serving a prison sentence for petty robbery—the last of several terms in prison he'd had in his lifetime. If Grace was honest with herself she would have to admit that her life was better without him.

She got down from the running board of the truck before Carl could come around and help her. She hefted Maria down as well, and motioned her toward the house.

The front-door lock was balky, as usual. Grace tried to think of anything at all she would miss about this rattletrap farmhouse. She couldn't come up with anything. Once she got the door unlocked, she turned to Carl. "Do you want me to make sure the car will start so that you can go back to town?"

"No." He shrugged. "What would I do there except sit in the house with the dog for company? Surely I can do something around here to help out."

"I imagine you can," she told him. "There's a few plastic crates upstairs in the children's rooms. Why don't you and Matt gather their toys and books and things and pack them in those, all right?"

It wouldn't take long. The milk crates had served as shelves in the bedrooms, and there wasn't much in either room that really belonged to the Mallory family.

"Is there anything in the garage besides the car?"

"Just some boxes. One or two with stuff in them that I never got around to unpacking, and a few empties. I'll need the empty ones in a while," Grace said.

"Good. Hand me your car keys and I'll go out and make sure the car's running. Then I'll bring the boxes in, all right?"

"Fine." Grace concentrated on coaxing the ancient furnace into putting out some heat. "Come in later and get warm. I don't want you catching pneumonia on my account." She fiddled with the thermostat until a groan from the basement told her that the furnace was coming to life. Then she went into the kitchen and started putting things on the table that she'd pack in the boxes Carl brought in.

There wasn't much. She had a sparse set of dishes, the kind collected from the grocery store week by week. Three pots, a teakettle and a large cast-iron skillet made up the entire pots-and-pans section.

The skillet was her favorite. It had been Jo's— probably even handed down from her mother or mother-in-law. Grace could remember being taught to cook, standing over this skillet. Jo had insisted that she take it with her after her quick wedding to Matt at seventeen. At least then, they hadn't moved far, and Matt had stayed out of trouble for a while. Jo had seen little Matt several times after his birth. It hurt Grace's heart, knowing that Jo had never seen Maria.

Maybe this move would be a new start in more ways than one, Grace reflected. She could start out fresh with so many things. She could take Carl up on his offer to go to church with him, maybe even talk to the pastor before that. And maybe she would find Jo. She wouldn't be returning to her a success. "More like a miserable failure," Grace said aloud to the half-empty kitchen. But somehow she knew Jo wouldn't mind. Just seeing her and two healthy children would bring a light to the older woman's eyes. Grace began to look forward to seeing that light.

"Thank you. Please add that to my bill." Didn't the woman know any other way to express gratitude? Probably not, Carl reflected as he surveyed himself in the mirror. He'd nicked himself shaving. Naturally, when he was taking Grace and the kids to church for the first time, he'd do that.

Carl was concerned about Grace. She seemed tired and worried all the time, at the end of her rope. It showed in the lines etched in her pale face, and in the shadows under her brown eyes. The tis-sue-paper-thin skin there looked dark with fatigue.

Surely she couldn't hold in the worry forever. Those feelings had to come out sometime. Proba-bly sometime soon, if she started feeling safe. Carl knew that when she did let go it would be complete for a little while. And from what he'd seen so far of Grace Mallory, it would not be in public. She wasn't a woman to share her emotions.

Not even when he'd insisted, first thing on the twenty-sixth, that she come to the store and they find her a pair of shoes that fit. Carl didn't even have to argue; she'd wordlessly followed him over there, with the children in tow.

It took only about two minutes to find boots that fit Matt. The boy seemed satisfied to know that he'd be working in the store and would earn his new boots. For his mother, it was different. Grace Mallory had narrow, delicate little feet that matched the rest of her body, and again Carl felt this crazy need to get all protective around her.

Finding shoes for Grace really only took a min-ute or two longer than fitting her son, but Carl's discomfort in doing the job stretched things out in his mind until it seemed like hours. And then all she could say was that, "Thank you. Please add them to my bill." Didn't anything ever rattle the woman? Bring her feelings to the surface?

Her kids, Carl decided. He'd have to watch

when she talked about them the next time. Perhaps then he would learn the key to that precious spot—wherever it was—that she had locked up in her heart. It amazed Carl that each day he spent around Grace made him more anxious to find that spot.

Pastor Peterson was nice. Welcoming and friendly—not what Grace expected when she told him before services that it had been nearly a decade since she'd been in a house of worship. "We hope you'll join us here often. And bring the kids to Sunday school," he told her. "They look about the age of a couple of mine, although Maria will be disappointed, because Todd's a boy. When you're six that's not appealing, is it?"

It surprised her that the pastor remembered her name, and the children's, so quickly. She wasn't sure why it surprised her even more that he was a normal person with four rowdy boys who jostled around in the crowded hallway outside his office with a bunch of other kids.

What surprised her still more was that the biggest kid in the hallway seemed to be Carl. Around the children and teenagers he came to life in a way that she hadn't seen before. She wondered if he was active with the youth here. If he wasn't, the church was missing something, Grace thought.

The inside of the church itself was quiet and calm. A huge pine tree filled the stone sanctuary with a light and wonderful green scent. The ornaments on it were different, and all seemed to have some Christian symbolism about them. There weren't many on the tree, and there were large gaping spots where things seemed to have been removed. Grace made a note to ask Carl about it later.

For now she sat quietly, wondering at the pain she suddenly felt. Being in a church—any church—made her think of Matt. It had been his decision that she wasn't to step foot in one—with him or without him—after they were married. Grace had always wondered what had happened that made him so angry with God that he would do anything to avoid Him.

She didn't know much about Matt's life before he'd drifted into hers when he was nineteen. He didn't talk about his family much except to say that he had left for good. From what little he'd said about fatherhood, Grace had thought she knew what his childhood had been like, and she had wanted to make their life together happy.

Still, Grace ached more over the loss of Jo than Matt, and felt Jo's absence from her life far more deeply.

If she had been more self-confident at seventeen, she probably wouldn't have married Matt Mallory. And if Jo had seen more of him before he insisted on running off to get married, Grace knew now that she never would have let the awkward young man "steal" her away. She wanted Jo, wanted her fiercely. But Matt had cut off contact with her after they'd moved away. He'd had a fit of anger like no other when he'd come out of jail the first time and had learned that Grace was still writing to her aunt. When Grace had finally summoned the courage and phoned Jo four years ago, the stranger who'd answered had no idea who Jo Sparks was, much less what had happened to her.

Grace feared that Matt had hidden a final letter—one from one of Jo's neighbors, telling her that her aunt had died. Matt's meanness would have let him keep a letter like that from her and bring it out only long afterward when liquor would have made him evil. Except he'd gone back to jail again and never come out, and Grace was left just not knowing.

That was what started the tears now—thinking of Jo and feeling sure she'd never see her again. The children stared at her, and Carl looked uncomfortable, but Grace couldn't stop crying. She knew it looked odd, surrounded by people singing happy Christmas carols. Let it look odd, she decided. After a few moments, Carl reached into one of his jacket pockets and pulled out a rumpled but clean handkerchief. "And don't tell me to add it to the bill," he growled in a low whisper as he handed it to her. Grace didn't know what made her more embarrassed—crying in church or laughing through her tears at what Carl had said.

After the service the pastor's wife came over and introduced herself. And like her husband, Barb Peterson wouldn't take no for an answer. So Grace found herself and the children having lunch at the parsonage along with Carl and more boys than she knew the Petersons called their own. "It happens this way every week," Barb told her. "The guys all want to bring a friend home after services. I usually plan on at least a dozen for Sunday lunch."

The thought of eating still made Grace's throat close. She fussed over the children—little Matt in his white shirt, looking as if he wanted to tease the collar open, and Maria, solemn and shy, in her one good dress. She looked as if she'd rather be home with her kitten than have people crowded around her. "Soon," Grace whispered to her as she bent to smooth the girl's hair. "We'll go home soon."

How quickly Grace had taken to calling Brenner's house "home." It felt so much more like one than the ramshackle farmhouse ever had. Still, the house screamed out for some attention in ways only a woman would notice. Grace was already itching to open windows and drag curtains outside to the clothesline the first day it got warm enough. Grace wondered what Carl Brenner would do when he saw his curtains on the line.

As if he'd read her mind, he turned and looked

at her. Grace found her face warming under his questioning gaze. She glanced down quickly so as not to confront the half scowl he'd turned at her, as if he'd caught her whistling in church. How could he possibly have known her thoughts?

Maybe he hadn't, Grace told herself. Maybe he'd just seen a woman staring at him and, tired of being looked at, he'd stared back. Maybe, like Maria, he just wanted to go home.

Grace took up her plate, where she'd rearranged half a sandwich so that it looked at least nibbled on, and thanked Mrs. Peterson again for the invitation.

Hal Peterson, who'd traded his formal black shirt and clerical collar for a sweater, came over to talk to Matt. "You guys going to walk to school, now that you're living in town? Todd and Josh could always use friends to walk with."

Grace stalled for a minute before looking at Carl. She hadn't discussed this with him yet. "Sure will," he said, getting up. "On days it's warm enough. You folks got a car pool going when it's really nasty out?"

The pastor nodded. "With four, we're almost our own car pool. Of course, this year the older two are both in high school, so the car situation gets touchy once in a while. We'd welcome somebody to trade off with." He leaned over to Maria. "You could be the rose among the thorns."

Grace could feel Maria shrinking beside her. "What does that mean, Mama?" she whispered.

"It means we will have to make all these wild boys behave around you. And it will do them good, Miss Maria," Hal Peterson told her.

"Oh. Good. I don't like thorns. They stick."

Hal Peterson laughed, gently. "All right. Well, we'll see you, then. And Mrs. Mallory? If there's anything else we can do, just let us know." The pastor smiled, extending a hand.

Grace thanked him and left quickly before tears overwhelmed her again. Outside she helped Maria into the back seat, and climbed into the front herself.

Matt climbed into the back next to Maria. "I like Josh. He's in my class. You meant what you said back there, about walking to school with him, and riding, maybe?"

"Every word. And no helping me in the store until the homework is done after school, got that?" Carl said to Matt, swinging around to face him while he backed out of the parsonage driveway.

"Yes, sir." Matt seemed to be as surprised as Grace. His father hadn't been fond of letting the kids have friends. And later, Grace had needed Matt to come home from school to watch his sister while she worked. She could see that living in town, with her working just five blocks from home, was going to open a different world for the boy.

"Thank you," she whispered. It was the first prayer she'd said in a long time that hadn't been desperately asking for something, and it felt very, very good.

Chapter Seven

Surveying the loaded truck bed on Monday morning, Grace told herself that it would take a month of Sundays, going to church each and every one of them, to pay back Barb Peterson for the help in moving. Not only had she brought a Crock-Pot full of soup to Carl's for the evening when everyone would be tired from moving, but she'd also lent them her oldest son, Jon, a strapping sixteen-year-old. He stood in the truck bed, loading furniture as Carl hoisted from the ground.

Grace felt more than ready to move her things by the time Carl had arrived with the truck. At first it had seemed rushed to go in and have everything removed before a new lease would have started on January first, but now Grace realized the wisdom of the plan.

As early as she could get everybody going that Monday, she and the kids had headed out to the farm. They'd worked the whole morning to pack what hadn't been packed before, take apart the two beds that belonged to them, and bundle up the linens.

Not that there was all that much to load. Most of the furniture in the house had belonged to the Kriegers. Grace wouldn't miss any of their things much. None of it had the homey feel of things Grace had owned forever. It was just stuff that someone else had left behind.

What Carl and Jon were putting on the truck would not have been worth much to anybody else, but it was precious just the same. Her rocker, which had held both her children as she'd soothed them to sleep as infants. The beds. One chest of drawers that had been in her bedroom. A family Bible, a couple of other books, and a very few odds and ends rounded out all her worldly goods. The children's clothes and toys were already at Brenner's.

Loaded in the back of a truck it didn't look like much. There should have been more, but Grace had never had the time or money to collect much.

While Carl and Jon loaded the bed frames, Grace went back into the house. There were floors to sweep and vacuum. She set Matt to cleaning the bathroom and let Maria walk around with a spray bottle wiping down the walls for stray fingerprints while she worked in the kitchen with a broom.

When everything was clean, Matt looked like he was ready to wilt, and Maria's hair seemed to indicate she'd been pulled through a fence backward. Grace herded them into the bare kitchen and laid out the sandwiches she'd packed, thankful she had remembered paper plates.

When Carl came in, he had a small cooler with him. "Stopped and bought some cold milk this morning. I even got those plastic quart bottles because I heard from somebody at Jon's house that he drinks from the container when nobody's looking. So I got him his own."

The teenager grinned sheepishly, but Grace noticed he didn't deny anything, either. Once more, Grace was struck by how well Carl related to kids. Carl passed the cooler to Jon, who seemed to down half the bottle of milk in one gulp. Grace was relieved that she'd packed double the sandwiches she'd thought they'd need. Carl and Jon, apparently the boy in town most likely to outstrip Carl in height, each put down three without blinking. Maria sat on the floor and looked at Jon with open admiration. "You're big," she told him.

"Naw." Carl leaned on the boy and upset his balance. "He's not that big yet, Miss Maria." She giggled at them roughhousing in front of her.

"Why, he isn't all that much bigger than your brother."

Maria giggled again. "Oh, yes, he is. Look at how tall he is."

"Yes, but look at little Matt." Carl's brow furrowed. "We aren't going to be able to call you that much longer, son. That 'little' part is going to have to go."

Matt hadn't looked up from his sandwich until now. Grace ached for him. She couldn't find a way to tell Carl how being made the center of attention affected her shy boy. She knew by the color of the back of Matt's neck under his pale hair that he wished he could vanish beneath the floorboards.

Still Carl persisted, oblivious. "Put your hand out here, Matthew. Look at what I'm talking about." The boy's gaze stayed on the floor, but his hand came out. Carl directed the bulky teenager to spread out his fingers palm to palm with the boy's.

"See, the hands and the feet, they grow first. And Matt isn't that far behind Jon, here. He's going to be one big boy in a couple of years. That's why I'm letting him work in the store," he said, mostly to Jon. "I figure if I train him early, he'll be able to do most of the heavy work by the time he's your age."

Matt went from looking at the floor to looking at his hand. Grace wanted to tell him that Carl was right. His long, bony fingers weren't that much smaller than the hands of the older boy beside him. But she stayed silent, letting her son figure it out for himself.

As he did, his shoulders straightened. "See, Mom. I told you that you should have let me help load the truck."

"Was she the one keeping you back?" Carl demanded. "If I'd known that, I would have said something. When we get to the other end, you get the boxes, all right?"

Matt nodded. "Yes, sir. Next time I will."

"Good. Now, how about putting on your jacket again and helping with those mattresses? They have to be fit in between the other stuff. Then we'll be done, and we can go."

Matt nodded. He watched Jon tip his milk bottle up and take a last swig. The younger boy lifted the jug at him wordlessly, and took one quick swig himself, backhanding a milk mustache from his face in the manner of his new idol. Then Matt, Jon and Carl headed up the stairs. Grace could have sworn she saw an identical swagger in all three backsides.

Later, as she stood outside, with the kids already in the truck and her furniture, such as it was, in the back, Grace looked at the house. "Sure you don't need any more time inside?" Carl asked.

Grace shook her head. "There's nothing here

I'm leaving behind.'' Tears sprang to her eyes as she said it, betraying her feelings.

"No? Then why are you upset?"

"Because now nobody will ever know how to find me. This is the last address anybody has for me. I haven't talked to my family in years, but I've always known we could probably find each other if we had to. Except now I know we can't. I can't be at least.''

Carl shook his head. "Moving the five miles or so into town doesn't have to change that. You ever heard of Internet searches for people?"

Grace looked at him, puzzled. "No. What would that do?"

Carl was grinning. And now, looking at him this closely, she could see what she'd wondered about before. His eyes were gray—not a dark, forbidding gray, but a blue-gray with almost the gleam of pewter or silver. Definitely a precious metal. "That, my friend, would find just about anybody in the United States that's alive and has an address or a telephone that's got a listed number."

Grace felt a hope stirring in her that she hadn't felt in a very long time. "Do you know anybody who does that?"

"You're looking at somebody. It's my hobby, you might say.''

A stray breeze picked up a strand of Grace's hair and tugged it away from her face. Her spirits lifted with it. She liked this feeling of hope. It was a new feeling, and she definitely liked it.

Grace stared down at her figures, wanting to wince. It was going to take more than a month to pay Carl Brenner back. She should be happy and comfortable. This time of day she had the house almost to herself. Dinner simmered on the stove, Maria and the kitten, which she'd named Fluff, played in a corner while Grace sat at the table looking at a piece of paper covered with numbers. The numbers didn't make her happy.

Even the list she'd added up didn't really compute to what she knew she owed Brenner already. He insisted that even though he was feeding and housing three of them, their board shouldn't count. Carl argued that he was saving more money not driving through fast-food places with Grace cooking all the time. According to him, groceries for four still put him ahead financially. It didn't seem right to Grace, but she'd learned to stop arguing with him unless it really mattered. Even then, it felt like arguing with a wall. So far, she hadn't found a point Carl Brenner was willing to concede in an argument. Maybe she just wasn't used to arguing anymore.

With Aunt Jo, arguing had always been a sport. It had been meant in good humor mostly, as a way to pass the time. Grace suspected it had been a ploy to get her to talk when she was a teenager. If so, it had worked. But arguing hadn't worked with Matt. He'd solved arguments physically.

So Grace had gotten out of practice, which was a shame because Carl Brenner seemed to be a champion arguer. Or at least a champion argument-winner. And not because he threatened to use his larger bulk to make a point, either. He just sat stolidly at the table and said his piece. And Grace let him win.

Of course, he was paying her. So she probably should let him win. But it didn't seem fair to Grace that he fed and housed three people and got precious little in return. She'd worked in the store the hectic week after Christmas for a few hours each day, training. It hadn't been difficult, and Carl professed that it had helped him.

As far as Grace could tell, he didn't really need help in the store that much. She felt more useful keeping house. When school started up again Matthew spent most of his time at school, or doing homework at the kitchen table, then maybe running back to the store for an hour. Maria didn't have much homework, being in first grade. At six she was starting to be a help, but mostly she sang to the cat. The cat loved it, but that didn't get any housework done.

Grace reveled in Maria's singing. For the first few days after they'd moved to town, she'd continued to say little. She was still getting well, and getting used to a strange place. Then slowly she began to talk more, and one morning Grace stopped in the middle of dusting the parlor when she heard a strange noise. She couldn't quite figure what the high sound was until she went closer to the kitchen and heard the strains of some ballad on the radio being mangled by her daughter.

Since then, the kitten had been treated to every song that Maria knew, plus a few Grace wondered where she'd picked up. Her shrill voice lacked a sense of rhythm, but she sang anyway. If Fluff would listen to that, she could, too.

Maria had her little chores, but they didn't amount to much in the scheme of things. Like any small child, she required as much chasing after and taking care of as she gave back in the way of help. And that was on good days. Still, Carl insisted on bringing home little things from the store or from Doc's for her and little Matt, and got frosted when Grace tactfully tried to tell him that she couldn't afford the treats.

"I didn't ask you to pay for them," he told her repeatedly with a glare that seemed to be more anger at being caught than anything else. He wouldn't have dreamed of giving out free merchandise to his other customers. Why her children? And why did he get so aggravated when they ate in the kitchen instead of the dining room with him?

Still, that arrangement had only lasted for about three days. On the fourth evening Carl had started a parade back into the kitchen with his dishes as quickly as she'd carried things into the dining room. After a third trip, she'd conceded and they'd eaten at the kitchen table together, no one speaking much. When he'd come home the next evening and seen Maria setting four places in the kitchen, the grunt as he'd taken off his boots had seemed to be one of satisfaction. It had been done his way ever since.

So he'd won his arguments. Grace, however, couldn't win much of anything. The paper in front of her told her that by the middle of February she would be at a point where she didn't owe Carl anything. Of course, that was counting on her getting her deposit back from Jake Krieger; and while the young man was honest, he wasn't good with finances.

Her calculations also left out some things Grace had to admit were important, like the cost of starting over anywhere that wasn't partially furnished. And the kids were both growing; last year's spring and summer clothes weren't going to fit.

She was still sitting there, figuring it all out, when Carl came in for dinner. He and little Matt burst in the door together, oblivious to the mud they tracked in until she pointed it out; then neither of them was terribly repentant. "It's warm out there," Carl said. "Spring just around the corner. Of course there's going to be mud."

"There's got to be cleaning, too," Grace replied, trying not to grumble as she got up and gathered her figuring. "Maria, set the table. Matt, take off those boots and then wash your hands."

"Guess that holds for me, too," Carl joshed, coming right behind her and looking straight down. What had gotten into him to make him this cheerful?

"I can't tell you what to do. It's your house." Grace swung by him and went to dish up the potatoes and the steak and gravy that had been stewing for hours. As she ladled the meat and gravy into the bowl, Carl's nose was twitching more than the kitten at her feet. She had to laugh, watching him, obviously in rapture over the smell of plain steak and gravy.

"Who fed you before?"

"Nobody except me. And I never learned to cook quite like that," he said. "There are days when I catch myself almost running home for dinner. Of course, I guess I need to run if I want to beat this one here to the table." He was reaching out to ruffle Matt's hair and seemed to be amazed when the boy scowled and ducked away from him. Grace gave her son a warning look and once again they ate in relative silence, Matt bolting a small portion of food, jamming his boots on and vanishing before Carl could say much of anything.

Maria, sensing the tension, ate quickly and excused herself after clearing her place. Grace knew she would go upstairs to hide under the covers of her bed, just to get away from what she felt down in the kitchen. Only Carl stayed at the table, and he looked stunned.

"What did I do?" His hushed question was full of pain.

"Nothing you shouldn't have."

"That's not true. That boy jumped almost as if I'd shot him." He looked down at his plate, stirring around the remains of his dinner. Getting up, he scraped it into the dog's bowl and whistled for Four. Grace had almost forgotten that the yellow dog had come in with the man and boy earlier, but he seemed happier to see the leftover steak than anyone at the table had been.

Grace tried to find a way to explain Matt. "You didn't do anything wrong, really. It's just that, well, Matt's daddy didn't call attention to him much. And when he did, it meant trouble. So he's not used to friendly teasing. Especially not from someone he admires."

Carl swung around from watching the dog eat and his gray eyes held real pain now. "It's my fault. I don't know how to act around him and the little girl. I didn't exactly have a normal childhood myself, and I've forgotten what it's like to be a kid.''

"I don't think so," Grace said softly. "I think you remember all too well."

Carl's face clouded over even more. "Maybe you're right. But I still messed things up." He stormed out of the kitchen, slamming the door shut behind him, leaving the confused dog still standing over his dinner bowl.

He had been angry. As angry as Grace had ever seen Matt. But he didn't swear, and he didn't hit. And he was angry not at her, or little Matt, but at himself, and at the world in general that let little boys go through the pain of growing up. Grace could feel herself trembling—partly in fear and partly in wonder.

The fear came from all the times she'd witnessed anger and borne the brunt of it. The wonder was a new thing, blooming like a flower. Carl showed her real, righteous anger over anybody not caring for a child. He had promised to take care of them all— as easily as Matt would have promised to slap her.

Then, with all that anger racing through him, flushing his face and balling up his fists, Carl walked away. Without hurting anybody. Was this his faith at work? If so, Grace wanted a share of that faith. She could see him outside the window, striding purposefully up the street. In a little while he would catch up with the hurrying smaller figure ahead and amaze him with what Grace already knew he would say.

A sheaf of white on the floor caught her eye. Carl's door slamming had pushed a breeze through the kitchen, blowing Grace's papers with their careful figures into a heap beside the dog still finishing his food.

She picked up the pages of calculations. She could probably use them to light the fireplace later—because suddenly she wasn't worried about overstaying her welcome here. Suddenly she had more important problems to solve, and all of them seemed to require her staying in this house. Here she had a child just learning to sing and one who needed to learn to be teased. And somehow she had realized that no matter how long she worked at paying Carl Brenner back, she would always owe him more than she could ever repay.

Chapter Eight

Grace had a headache. She seemed to have one perpetually these days. Probably from Kayla's constant chatter. The young woman had taken to coming to Carl's straight from class at the junior college and staying until just before dinner. She'd flit out the door, timing her disappearance to avoid Carl and manage to get home just before her father.

Grace wasn't sure if it was her company or her instruction that Kayla craved. With no mother living, the girl had nobody to teach her how to do things around the house, so she spent as many afternoons as Grace would let her underfoot in Carl's kitchen, hanging about and talking constantly. Today Grace had put her to work, peeling apples for three pies. Grace had thought that would slow down her tongue, but it didn't. Not nearly enough, anyway.

"I think black is my favorite color. Dad says it's not a color at all. If it's not, I guess my favorite is teal. How about you?" For what, Grace had no idea. She'd been too busy trying to triple her pie-crust recipe in her head to pay attention.

"I'm sorry. Color for what?"

Kayla giggled. "Anything. I love the sound of the name. Teal. What's your favorite color?"

"Don't have one." Grace measured salt into the cupped palm of her left hand. Too much? Enough? She added a tiny bit more and poured it into the bowl with the flour. Creaming in the shortening, she could hear Kayla sighing. "Now what's the matter?"

"Everybody has a favorite color. How can you not have one?"

"Haven't thought about it in a long time. I've got more to do than wonder what my favorite color is. Besides, what good is it?"

Kayla's perfect brow furrowed and she spluttered. "Well, lots of good. When somebody wants to buy you a new car, they know what color to buy if they know you have a favorite color. Or if you're going to buy yourself a new top…"

"I haven't ever had anybody buy me a car, new or otherwise, Kayla." She tried to say it without sighing. "And when I need clothes I tend to buy them on sale, or at a resale shop. Color doesn't much matter.''

"Oh. Well, I still like black. And teal." Kayla went back to peeling the apples.

Grace felt badly about snapping at the girl. She couldn't help sounding so witless. Kayla just loved to talk, and she had nobody at home to talk to. Getting the tiny hand grater, she grated a little nutmeg and cinnamon into the pie dough, then started stirring in cold water until the dough balled up.

"Why did you do that? Stir in the spices, I mean. I thought they just went in the filling."

"Usually they do. But since I have them, I figured why not use them," Grace explained, gathering up the dough to cool for a few minutes in the refrigerator before she rolled it out. She didn't explain to Kayla that cooking in Carl's kitchen felt like heaven. After years of making do with whatever scraps she had on hand, having a widely stocked pantry and time to use it made her feel exuberant. So did having an enthusiastic Carl to feed three times a day.

Besides, she wanted supper tonight to be special. It was the beginning of her plan to pay Carl back for all he'd been doing for her family. She figured his own apple pie would be a start. He'd hinted at Christmas that he could put away one on his own.

"Now, let's put sugar and flour on those apples to draw some juice," she told Kayla, leaning over her. "Then you're going to learn to roll out a crust." Kayla groaned. This should keep her quiet for a few minutes, Grace thought; a tongue poking out of the corner of one's mouth for concentration could not be used for talking.

The house smelled wonderful. Kayla, packed off with her first homemade pie, vowed that she would send her father over to talk to Grace if he didn't believe she'd made it herself. Grace didn't relish talking to Larry Trent, but she would back up his daughter. The girl needed a mother, Grace thought again. A mother would have taught her all the things she was lacking. A mother would also point out to Larry that Bill Parker needed to stay away more or have more supervision when he was at the Trents' house. As it was, Grace figured Larry was probably so happy to have someone else dealing with his chatterbox daughter that those two didn't get the supervision they needed.

It would take more than his own apple pie to get Carl in the mood to listen to a plan to chaperon Kayla and Bill. Even Grace knew not to attempt that. So Grace quietly put supper on the table and stood watching her family settle in.

It was evident by the time Carl and Matt came home for supper that Carl had patched things up with her son. Grace itched to ask him how, but she knew better. Neither of those quiet, prickly males would take kindly to her knowing about their private conversations. She just had to be happy with the fact that they were speaking to each other in a limited way, using the little half bath off the kitchen to wash up together and seeming to get along.

Her traitorous fingers wanted to touch Carl more and more often. He seemed to invite her touch just by his very presence. The way his hair curled softly at the back of his collar made her want to twine her fingers there and stroke. The set expression around his mouth made her want to trace the lines away. The lines would fall away, too, if she just put one finger there and drew it down the side of his face.

Sometimes now it took all her willpower to remind herself that Carl was not for the touching, no matter how tempted she was. She was a widow with two children to support, and Carl was her employer. Nothing more.

Maria pulled on her sleeve, demanding attention. "Mama! You're always telling us to sit down while it's still hot. How come you're still standing?"

Grace felt her cheeks warming. "Just daydreaming, I guess. Your turn to give thanks, sugar." The table talk picked up again the moment Maria finished, and Grace was saved from any more deep thoughts about her predicament by making sure everyone had bread and neither child upset their milk.

She'd baked him his own pie. Carl was so touched by that little gesture. True, the apples and flour and everything else had come from his grocery shopping. Still, that pie cooling on the countertop with a C cut in the top instead of the usual little chicken-track vent marks moved him—maybe because no one else in Redwing would have thought of it.

No one else anyplace would have thought of it, Carl admitted to himself. He probably couldn't come up with the names of five human beings who cared if he lived or died. Larry might miss the convenience of the store, perhaps. And Doc wouldn't have anyone to debate with. But truly miss him? Not likely. Only Four—hunkered in his corner, basking in the reflected warmth of the kitchen, would care. And now, perhaps, Grace and the children. And maybe even that stupid kitten— as far as cats cared, which didn't appear to be much.

With each passing day it got harder not to stare at Grace across the table. Each day, even each meal, she seemed to be more at home in his house. Little things were rearranged here and there to prove that she'd touched them far more than he ever had. Things he hadn't ever thought of cleaning had been scrubbed, polished, waxed or shone.

It had never occurred to Carl that the tops of door frames were objects to dust. He wondered how Grace got that high. Probably dragged a kitchen chair around the house. Over his dinner he envisioned her in his bedroom, standing on that kitchen chair, reaching up to work on the top of the door frame. Her slight figure would be enhanced by her lifting her arms over her head. He imagined her high squeal when he stood behind her and gently clasped his hands around her rib cage, then lifted her down from the chair.

She would be warm in his arms, and smell of roses. He could turn her around in his hands as easily as he could handle the kitten. Knowing Grace, though, she'd probably whop him on the head with whatever she was using to dust that door frame.

Grace spoke and reality washed over him like a cold bucket of water. "Something wrong with dinner?" Grace asked, pushing away his lovely daydream. She had little puckers of concern between her eyebrows. "You feeling all right?"

"Fine." It came out more harshly than Carl had intended. "Just...thinking about the store accounts." What a lame excuse for where his thoughts had been.

Carl wasn't proud of those thoughts. Especially

when they concerned a widow with two little kids. She'd shown no indication that she felt anything but gratitude for having a roof over her head and kind treatment. It would be ridiculous to assume anything more just because she'd baked him an apple pie. He glanced over at the dog, searching for something—anything—to bring into the conversation.

When he looked closely at Four, he saw at least one reason for the big animal's expression of bliss. Instead of his normal patch of floor, the dog seemed to be stretched out on a blanket. "Making a bed for the dog now?"

Grace seemed abashed. "I found that blanket in one of the chests, full of moth holes. I couldn't patch it. So I folded it and bound the edges. He looks cold sometimes." Four's heavy tail thumped as if he agreed with her and knew what she'd said.

"All right. But no bows tied around his ears or anything."

"I wouldn't dream of it." There seemed to be a giggle buried just under the surface of her reply. For the life of him, Carl couldn't look at Grace again for the rest of the meal. If he did she'd surely see his embarrassment over thinking he'd been given special treatment, then realizing that even the dog got special treatment around here.

He ate half the pie. Grace knew the man had an appetite, but even she was amazed. Her husband had never eaten that much at one meal in his life. She got pure joy now out of watching Carl eat.

In fact, Grace had to admit that she got joy out of watching this man, period. Each day the image of the lonely little boy he'd described receded a little into the background. His large frame and that tiny bit of a scowl that seemed to be a constant part of expression made him seem anything but boyish.

It was good to see him without the scowl as he told little Matt how good his mom's pie tasted. A fact that Matt wasn't disputing, having eaten a second piece himself. Granted, beside what Carl had eaten, his pieces had looked like slivers. For a brief flash Grace could envision the two of them years into the future, both eating like truck drivers. It would be a challenge to feed them.

Maria dropped her fork. The noise shook Grace out of her fantasy. She wouldn't be here in a couple of years. She probably wouldn't be here longer than a few months. By the time the school year finished, she'd be settled somewhere else, away from Carl.

She couldn't stay. Not if she wanted to keep out of trouble. Because as Carl looked less boyish every day, he looked more manly. More in need of her touch. It would be so easy to walk over to where he sat enjoying that pie and run her fingers around his collar at the nape of his strong neck. So easy and yet so dangerous because of the temptation it would stir up.

Carl's voice as he talked to little Matt pulled Grace back to reality. "We going to study after dinner?"

"Yes, sir," Matt said hurriedly, sliding off his seat. "At least I think so. I better go check."

Carl smiled. "And you, Miss Maria. There's a brand-new pencil on my desk in the parlor, and a piece of paper. How about you go practice your letters with that for a while, all right?" Maria nodded and dashed off, as well. Maria never needed any urging to write or draw. Carl seemed to understand that while her shyness around him continued, her natural love of writing and drawing won her over when he encouraged her. Slowly but surely he charmed her to him, one piece of paper at a time.

Grace wondered why he wanted to be alone with her. And wondering pushed her into nervous movement. "More coffee?"

"I'll take one more cup. I'm stuffed as it is, but I still want to sit awhile." He stretched luxuriously, reminding Grace of a large, just barely tame animal. She wondered if anyone else saw him the way she did. To everyone else was he just Carl the storekeeper—one of the many familiar folks in town? Did anyone else sense the restlessness just under his surface calm, see the bunched muscles that took hours to relax when he came home at night?

She poured his coffee, not daring to look into those gray eyes. One look would be all it would take tonight for her to start talking in earnest. Telling him why she'd baked him a pie, and how much she was touched by his caring.

"Could I have a spoon?" His voice was deceptively soft. Grace felt chagrined that she hadn't put spoons on the table. What kind of housekeeper forgot the spoons? How could a man stir his coffee after he added a little cream if he didn't have a spoon? Come to think of it, what had he been doing all through dinner?

Her haste made her clumsy. That and the fact that she still wasn't used to the dimensions of this room, the furniture in it, everything. Her mind still held the contours of that awful kitchen in the farmhouse. There had been so little to trip over that things here remained a hazard, especially the outsplayed legs of Carl's kitchen chairs.

She had been here three weeks, but she still caught herself on them several times a day as she went about the kitchen. This time, her ankle neatly hooked around the chair leg in her haste to get him a spoon. If the chair had been empty, she would have just barked her shin and knocked the chair over. Instead, Carl's solid bulk anchored his chair, which he'd pushed back a little from the table as he lazed over his coffee.

Grace plowed into the chair leg, and momentum kept her moving forward—forward as Carl's eyes widened and he flung up his hands to catch her. He caught her, all right, but the movement she'd already started carried her smack against his chest. The solid thud she made surprised both of them.

"Well, now." Carl's eyes widened in surprise, and he seemed intrigued to have an armful of her.

And being in Carl's arms was marvelous. Grace closed her eyes and leaned her head back, feeling time slip into slow motion.

Then suddenly, a commotion to end all commotions broke loose in the kitchen.

Chapter Nine

Grace watched as Carl paced the kitchen. She had just managed to soothe Kayla and wipe her teary face after she'd come bursting into the room. "He's gone!" she'd howled between sobs. "Bill's gone! And he didn't even taste my pie." Kayla now sat in the parlor, comforted by both children and the kitten. The dog would have nothing to do with her, and sat on his blanket in the corner, watching Carl pace.

Carl raked a hand through his dark hair, already rumpled in aggravation. "So why is Kayla so upset Bill left town? Is she— Aw, nuts, how do I put this so I don't offend you, or her? Did they—"

Grace tried not to purse her lips. "The only one offended seems to be you, Carl. If you want to know if Kayla is pregnant, the answer is no. Kayla may be young and impulsive, but she's not stupid. In a town this size, with her father the mayor and the banker, the boy would have been marched back to Larry's with a shotgun long ago if that had been the case.''

"Well, how could I know? She comes in here wailing like a banshee, and all. And she is young, and very naive and— I repeat, how could I know?''

He looked so upset that Grace almost felt sorry for snapping at him. Almost. The thought that he had just naturally assumed that about Kayla and Bill didn't amuse her. ''Why didn't you just figure that she wouldn't go that far with anybody, even Bill?''

He stopped pacing and looked at her with a pained expression. ''I should have, shouldn't I? But look at things my way, would you, Grace? He's a boy, really a young man. And I remember being a young man. If I'd had a girl like Kayla following me around town at his age, I would have tried.''

Grace stood. ''Oh, I expect he tried. But Kayla is smarter than you give her credit for and believes in the biblical promises about purity.''

He flashed her a quick, rueful smile. ''Good. It makes my job a lot easier if I'm going to find the kid if I don't have a seven-month deadline, and a guy who doesn't want to be found to begin with.''

Grace felt a thrill go through her. "Find him? You sound like you've done this before."

He shrugged his massive shoulders. "It's what I do nights when I should be working on the store accounts. I told you before. I find things. Or people. Some alive, some dead."

Her lips felt wooden as she kept speaking. "And you...have success at this?"

"Sometimes. Almost all the time, really. When I'm not looking for someone I want to find for myself, that is. The one time I tried it for me, it didn't work. But I learned enough to do it for other folks. One time I found a girl Hal baptized twenty years ago. Her folks were just passing through town, and he always wondered what became of her. She's living in Montana on some ranch, married to a cowboy and the mother of twins. Found them all last year. Hal was pleased as punch."

"So you can probably find Bill?"

"Oh, sure. Especially because he's only been gone since this afternoon. I've got a couple of ideas, anyway. With the young ones it's easy. Chances are good he's gone off to St. Louis or Memphis to seek his fortune so that he can be a self-made millionaire by Easter and come back and claim his ladylove."

Grace found herself giggling in spite of herself. Carl had come much closer to her during his last speech, and now they stood together in the middle of the kitchen, him with his hands on her shoulders.

"I like your laugh. Haven't heard enough of it."

"Not much to laugh about lately, I guess." Grace felt tongue-tied. He always had that effect on her when he looked down into her eyes and smiled.

There were words she wanted to say to Carl, here and now. But she didn't know how to ask. "Could you find someone for me? After Bill, I mean. Bill has to come first."

"Why?"

"Because. Kayla needs him to come back right away. She'll be crushed until you find him and get him home again. And I can wait."

"Can you?" His hand was warm on her cheek.

"If I have to." She sensed a current of meaning between them that went far deeper than the surface conversation. "I'm used to waiting."

Carl's brows drew together. "Used to coming last, you mean. I don't intend for it to be that way here, Grace."

She swallowed hard, wanting to lean her forehead against his broad chest and just stay. Instead, she kept looking into those pewter-colored eyes. "I know. And I'm so thankful for it. But Carl, we both have other things to do. I've got to get my children settled again, and you've got a store to run and plenty of other things on your mind. I know you'll find Jo for me when you can.''

Carl seemed to deflate a little, losing the masculine teasing arrogance. "This Joe. Would it be someone I'm going to resent the daylights out of once I find him?" His crestfallen look made Grace reach up to him and stroke his cheek, the way she'd caress one of the children.

"No. And it's *her*. Jolene Sparks, my aunt who raised me. I know she's out there somewhere. I'm almost sure of it. If she were dead…I'd know it.'' There, the most awful words had been said and she still stood.

"You're right. And we'll find her. I'll show you all my secrets for finding people. We can do it together.''

"But first you'll find Bill.''

Carl sighed and let go of her. "But first I'll find Bill. You are so stubborn, woman, I don't know what to do with you.''

Grace headed toward the parlor, looking back over her shoulder to have the last word. "For the present, Carl, that is a relief.''

After a little more discussion, Kayla was sent home to calm down and wait—a process Carl doubted she could accomplish. But he decided to give her the benefit of the doubt, and made a mental note to go over and talk to Larry at some length the next day when he hit a slow period at the store.

Grace busied herself tidying the kitchen for the last time that evening. She put out dough to rise for cinnamon rolls while Carl and Matt finally got to their studying together. Maria sat in the corner nearest the stove, close to Four, and rocked and sang to the cat. Kayla's outburst had upset her. Singing to the cat calmed her by the minute. Grace wondered again at her resiliency.

"Go up and lay out your clothes for tomorrow and come back down in your pajamas," Grace told her son. "I'll read to you both tonight before you go to bed." He seemed to be ready to argue for a moment, then squared his shoulders, nodded and went up the stairs while she put a towel over the sweet-roll dough.

"And you, miss," she said, turning to her daughter.

"Not loud. You'll wake Fluff," Maria said solemnly.

"All right." Grace spoke more softly. "Put Fluff down by the dog and go get your nightgown on, too. I'll braid your hair while we're waiting for your brother."

Alone in the kitchen, Grace savored the faint scent of cinnamon in the air. She gave her hands a last swipe with her damp work towel and went to hang it up on the back side of the pantry door.

This big house felt like a dream. She had anything she should need or want to cook or sew, or otherwise provide for her family. Grace wondered again at that part of the change in her life. How had it happened so quickly?

She felt like a bad person. Just as bad as Matt had always said she was. A good wife would be sorrier than this to be a widow and less relieved every morning to wake up alone except for a cat and Maria.

Her gladness still worried her. Surely her marriage hadn't been that different from other people's. Surely she should be as bereft as the young girl who'd left here in tears just because her boyfriend had skipped town. Perhaps if the Matt Mallory who had died had been that boyfriend of hers, so many years ago at Jo Sparks's home, she would have been bereft. Not anymore.

She turned out the kitchen lights, leaving a single bulb on over the stove. Carl still sat in the parlor, and she would go there to read her children a story. Something uplifting with a happy ending so that they would believe in a far different future than the only one she could see ahead of them.

The next morning Grace rose early, stirring before anyone else. She slid into her clothes as quietly as possible and went downstairs to bake the cinnamon rolls. She hoped she would do well with this batch. It had been a while since she'd baked them. At Jo's they had always been reserved for celebration days, and over the last few years there had been so little to celebrate.

Today felt like a celebration day. The silver-blue winter sunlight coming through the kitchen windows making the clean glass sparkle was like a blessing. Grace felt pride looking at that glass. She didn't think too many other people around the town of Redwing had taken advantage of last week's brief thaw to wash windows. Now, with the return of the icy cold, Carl's windows all sparkled.

The rolls had risen just the way she'd wanted. Fifteen minutes later the rolls were in the oven. Somehow she had been drawn back to the Word more often since she'd been in Carl's house. Was that because it seemed like a haven?

Though not the world's fastest reader, Grace didn't have to follow along on the printed page with her finger and sound things out. Instead, she had a good, steady rhythm that she'd forgotten how much she enjoyed. And Aunt Jo had always used this particular method to time her sweet rolls. She said if you left a pan in there long enough to really read a chapter in any of the Gospels, you would get a good brown finish on them, and have done something worthwhile yourself. Her oven timer had never worked, but that had never bothered Jo. She'd always had her backup "Bible timer."

Grace nearly jumped out of her skin when Carl cleared his throat behind her. She'd been so absorbed in the scents of cinnamon and sugar in the warming room and the words in the book before her that she hadn't heard him come in. She knew she probably looked as flighty as Kayla, with one hand pressed to her chest and sitting up poker straight, but she couldn't help it.

"Is this a private party, or can anyone join?" he asked.

"It's your house. How could I possibly exclude you from anything?" Grace fought hard to keep a level tone with no hint of a gasp.

Carl shook his head, making little waves of his dark hair bounce. He needed a haircut. "You haven't learned yet, have you, Grace? To go along with teasing. I always feel so mean when I tease you."

"Don't. I'm just not used to it much anymore." She got up from her place at the table. "The coffee should be ready, even if the rolls have a little while to go. Would you like a cup?"

"Sure would," he said, putting a hand on her shoulder. "And I can get it for myself. Even being the housekeeper doesn't call for you waiting on me hand and foot. Especially not when there's something that smells that good in the oven."

Grace felt herself blush. "All right." No sense arguing over things with Carl. So she sat down and went back to her reading. To time the rolls, she needed to finish the chapter.

Carl settled in beside her with his coffee. "Read it out loud, could you? I stayed up awhile after all of you went to bed last night, and I could use something stirring to get me all the way awake this morning."

She traced the tiny lines of print until she found her place again. "I don't know how stirring you'll find this. It isn't exactly a Gospel that will appeal to a storekeeper."

It was fun to watch his bemused expression as he tried to figure out what she meant. The further she read, the more he understood. "Luke, chapter twelve. I'm already about halfway through. Verse twenty-five. 'And which of you with taking thought can add to his stature one cubit? / If ye then be not able to do that thing which is least, why take you thought for the rest? / Consider the lilies how they grow: they toil not, they spin not; and yet I say unto you, that Solomon in all his glory was not arrayed like one of these. / If then God so clothe the grass, which is today in the field, and tomorrow is cast into the oven; how much more *will he clothe* you, O you of little faith?'" By the time she'd finished, Carl was laughing.

"I see what you mean. If my customers took that one to heart, I wouldn't sell much, now would

I? And I take it back. You do know what teasing is all about."

"Just rusty, I guess," Grace said, getting up to look at the rolls. Obviously she wasn't going to be able to sit quietly and read to time them. Carl's presence distracted her, made her want to get up and move. When she sat still she looked at him too much, thought about him even more. Neither led to her feeling calm.

The rolls still needed a few more minutes. The aroma filling the kitchen, and wafting up the stairs would draw the children soon. Grace figured they'd be downstairs ready to eat just about the time the rolls came out of the oven.

When he spoke again, it startled Grace so much she nearly slammed the heavy oven door. "Tell me about this aunt of yours. Why'd she raise you, anyway?"

"Because my mother couldn't. Jo was *her* aunt, really. My great-aunt. She'd raised Mama—what raising she got—and then Mama ran off at sixteen. A couple of years later she came back, pregnant and alone.

"Mama said my daddy had been killed in Vietnam, and she didn't know where else to go. Some folks said she didn't even know who my daddy was. Jo stopped that pretty quick. Mama stayed with Jo for a while after I was born. And even after she went back to wherever she'd gone in the first place, I remember her coming back. Until I turned four and she was in a car accident. I remember her being young and pretty, but not much else.''

Carl listened intently, nodding and sipping his coffee. It had been so long since anyone had wanted to know. Matt had never referred to her mother, except in an unkind way. He maintained that everybody in their small community had known Grace's mother was just a free-love flower child, and her daughter would follow in her footsteps; and that she should be grateful that he wanted to marry her.

Opening the oven door, she pushed that particular memory aside and pulled the pan out, moving quickly so as not to burn herself. She slid it onto the top of the stove, using folded towels as a cushion against the pan's heat. Working quickly and deftly, she put the sticky rolls on a plate.

''So your aunt—or great-aunt, I guess—how old would she be?''

Grace leaned back on her heels, calculating. ''Well past sixty. Probably about sixty-seven or sixty-eight.''

Carl looked thoughtful, serious. ''Do you have an address for her, someplace you know she's been lately?''

Grace sat down at the table, looking at the fine-grained wood of the surface. ''How lately? I haven't seen her since little Matt was two. And the last phone number I had for her doesn't work.''

Carl nodded. ''Could she have moved?''

''She could have. Or she could have died. Either way, it's pretty hopeless, isn't it?'' Grace let her shoulders droop. Carl put his coffee cup down with enough force to spill a little of the brown liquid onto the saucer.

''Don't say that. Not yet. I've found some pretty impossible folks in the last ten years. Maybe we can find your aunt for you, once I find Bill. You did want me to find him first, didn't you?''

''I guess I still do, for Kayla's sake. I can—''

''I know, Grace.'' He covered her hand with his larger one. ''You can wait. But I don't know how much longer I can.''

''Awhile, out of necessity, Carl.'' She withdrew her hand from under his warm, sheltering one. ''Those children are coming down for breakfast. I'm not likely to see you alone again all day.'' The surprise on his face was worth the effort Grace had to put forth to tease him. She might get the hang of this teasing thing yet.

Chapter Ten

It did not take long for Grace to decide that as much as she liked most of the store work, she despised inventory. She could see the reasons for it, but counting every item in the store was tedious, even with the little ticket scanner that Carl showed her how to use.

There were a lot of small items that weren't ticketed, like baby socks in the children's department, and almost everything in the Boy Scout case. For those, they had to use the old-fashioned method of one person calling out a name or stock number of an item, the other tallying how many there were. It took hours.

With each hour Grace spent in such close proximity to Carl Brenner, she got to know him better. The better she knew Carl, the better she liked him.

In fact, she had feelings that were more than just liking the man.

He was big and brash and good-looking—that part she couldn't deny. But that wasn't what drew her to him. It was the open, friendly way he dealt with all his customers, even though Grace could tell that running the store wasn't what he really wanted to do with his life. Even in the middle of inventory he stopped calmly to answer questions for fifteen minutes for one sweet older lady who ended up buying nothing, but now had her checking account straightened out, thanks to Carl's help.

Carl's talent was with people—that much Grace could tell already. And seeing him with all the different people he dealt with, she wondered why he hadn't ever considered the ministry. At the church he seemed to come alive, especially when he was with children and teenagers, who seemed naturally drawn to him.

"So, did you go to school to learn to do this?" Grace asked casually while they were counting Boy Scout items after the older lady had left.

"Sort of. My uncle sent me to college, anyway. I did two years in business, then came back here when he had a heart attack. That pretty much ended my formal education. He needed me to take over, so I did."

"Ever thought of finishing up?" Grace asked.

"I know I've always dreamed of just starting college myself."

"You'd be good at it," Carl said, making her shiver when he turned that silvery gaze on her. "Running the store here told me I wasn't going to finish up. Not in business, anyway."

There was something he hadn't said that Grace felt like pursuing. She wanted to know this man's hopes and dreams. But she couldn't bring herself to ask about them yet. It still felt like an intrusion into his life. Everything she'd seen so far had told her that Carl was a very private person, and as much as she cared for him, she couldn't breach that privacy yet.

But she wanted to. So much of this big man's heart was still a mystery, and day by day Grace wanted in on the secrets. What made him smile? What was he thinking when she caught him watching her those several times a day? Who, besides that magnificent dog, did he love and care for?

None of those questions were going to answer themselves. And Grace wouldn't get an answer from Carl on any of them right this moment because they had company in the store.

Grace looked up when the bell over the door rang. Naomi from the café bustled in with a covered plate. "Oatmeal cookies," she said. "I noticed the kids have taken to stopping here on their way home from school, and I thought you might want to have something for them.''

''And maybe for Carl?'' Grace added, unable to conceal a smile.

Naomi smiled back. ''Well, there is that. I know he likes cookies as well as the kids do.''

Grace took a deep breath. ''And you're grateful for him taking us in and talking to Matt so all the little goodies on your counter stopped disappearing,'' she said.

Naomi colored. ''I never would have said anything. I raised a couple of boys myself, and I know it happens sometimes, even when you're doing all you can.''

''It won't happen again,'' Grace told her, touched by the sympathetic light in Naomi's eyes. The woman could have said all kinds of awful things, but she hadn't. Maybe, Grace thought, she was going to have to revise her personal opinion of several people in town, not just Carl.

The man himself came in from the back room, his nose twitching. ''I heard the bell, but I didn't know it was you, Naomi. Especially not with fresh cookies.''

''You would have been out sooner, I'll bet,'' she said, her eyes bright. Carl nodded, and took a cookie from the plate on the counter.

''You can say that again. Once the schoolkids get in here these will be gone in a flash. I couldn't talk you out of about a quart of milk to go with them, could I?''

Naomi laughed. ''I should have just brought it along and saved myself the trip.''

''I'll go back with you and get it,'' Grace offered. ''It will give us a minute to talk.''

''Don't let her pay for that milk, Naomi,'' Carl called out as they went through the door. ''Put it on my account.''

''You're not going to listen to him, are you?'' Grace asked.

''I'd better. He's my best customer,'' Naomi said. ''Even though he's been eating at home a lot more, lately. You must be doing better in the cooking department than Carl ever did for himself.''

''I try. There aren't too many ways he'll let me pay him back,'' Grace admitted. She felt she could be more open with the older woman.

''He is stubborn and determined that way,'' Naomi agreed. ''Do you know that when Rafe Johnson broke his arm last winter that man insisted on running him a tab at the café every day? For the entire eight weeks he was in a cast? Said if we didn't have Meals-on-Wheels around here it was the least he could do for one of the old-timers. Of course, he didn't say that to Rafe.''

''I'll bet not,'' Grace said. ''Especially the 'old-timer' part.'' She was touched again by the way that Carl gave of himself to people. Maybe it should make her feel less special, that he seemed to do it for a lot of folks. Somehow she couldn't feel less special where Carl was concerned, though.

Grace got her quart of milk—or rather, Carl's quart of milk—and headed back to the store. The bell jingled for her just the way it jingled for anybody else when she came through the door. "Are we almost done with inventory?" she asked. "And even if we're not, do you want to stop for milk and cookies before the kids get here?"

"Yes, we're almost done," Carl said, with a brightness in his eyes. "I swear, this is like doing inventory with Kayla. You really don't like this part, do you?"

"Not at all. It seems like a bunch of busywork," Grace admitted. "I can't see the point to it."

"The point is that we have to know what sold and what didn't of the stuff I ordered last spring. We've got to replace what sold, and reduce the stock on what didn't so that I don't find myself swamped with the wrong stuff about next October," Carl said. "See, in a couple of weeks the reps are going to come in or call me, and I'm going to have to make decisions on next winter's stock."

"Next winter's?" Grace echoed. It made her head swim. "And I always thought it was awful that the stores got Christmas stuff in before Halloween. I didn't think about having to order it before Valentine's Day."

Carl shrugged. "Breaks of the game. You always have to be anticipating on several levels. But then that's just why I think you'd be better at this whole racket than I am."

"You think I anticipate better?" Grace asked, feeling puzzled.

"You have to," Carl said. "You've managed to raise two kids by yourself and keep all three of you going with next to nothing. That takes planning and anticipation no end. That or trusting in the Lord for everything."

"And you've seen enough of my life to know that I'm sorely lacking in the trust department," Grace said ruefully.

Carl's face changed instantly. "I didn't mean it that way, Grace, honest...."

"I know you didn't," she told him, eager to reassure him that her feelings weren't hurt. "But you can look at my life and tell that it's been a while since I've trusted anybody to provide for me, even God. I have you to thank for what trust I've regained."

"Really?" Carl stepped closer, almost close enough to touch her. Grace felt her mouth go dry. "Then we've both got something to be thankful for, I guess. Because I find that you and your kids add a dimension to my life that's been missing for a long time. Maybe it's *never* been there, really."

Grace didn't know what to say. It was a relief

when the bell jingled behind her and the kids poured into the store. Carl stepped back, the noise of several voices and several pairs of wet boots filled the area, and life went on as before.

"All right, cookies!" Matt crowed. "Where did you get these?"

"From Miss Naomi. She sent them over just for you," Carl told him.

"You and the rest of the kids, and Carl," Grace added. "So don't wolf them all down at once, okay?"

"Sure. You want one, Maria?"

"Sure," she echoed. Only a step behind him, Maria was taking off her coat and settling her book bag on the floor. Grace knew she should tell her to put her things in the back room right away, out of everyone's path. But it was so nice to watch her happy, glowing child come in from the cold, with cheeks red and a smile on her face. There would be time to correct her in a few minutes.

Maria had taken to wearing Grace's scarf to school with her coat instead of a hat. The big woolly scarf was also a rich, brilliant blue, and Grace knew it satisfied some need in her daughter to wear it. So she used an old hat herself, and knitted gloves. Maria had mittens, and the big woolly scarf, which made her sigh in contentment over its soft envelopment of her small body.

"Did you leave my kitty at home again?" Maria asked as she put part of a cookie in her mouth.

"We've been over this before," Grace replied, trying to sound stern. Leaving Fluff behind, even for a quick trip to town, had become an effort, but Grace had convinced her stubborn daughter that the half-grown cat had no desire to be stuffed into a carrier for the journey. She could just imagine explaining that one to Carl if they were to let the kitten roam around his store.

"All right." Maria took a cookie in each hand from the proffered plate, looking over her shoulder at her mother with a sly grin. No sense, Grace thought, in trying to tell her different. Carl would spoil her yet. She picked up the blue scarf from the floor where her daughter had dropped it. Maria had already headed for the stockroom, cookies in hand.

"Do you indulge in such things?" Carl asked, still holding out the plate.

"I don't know. Are they any good?"

"Probably not as good as yours," Carl said. "But the best around, otherwise."

Grace took a cookie from the plate. Solid and warm, it felt good in her hand. She bit into it, savoring the crisp outside and the soft, brown-sugar-flavored interior.

For a moment, childhood memories flooded back to her at the sharp sweetness. She had probably been no bigger than Maria when she'd come home from school to warm cookies. Jo hadn't ever had much around the place, but she'd found ways to make small treats for a lonely child.

Sometimes it would be cookies waiting after the walk from where the bus let them off; other times a scrap of cloth left over from dressmaking would have been magically transformed into a dress for Katherine, her doll. There were so many happy memories there when Grace chose to let them in.

The bell over Carl's door suddenly jingled again, bringing her back to the present and the rest of the cookie, still in her hand.

It was Tim Peterson, who seemed to be looking for Matthew. "Hey, Spence, want to come over and do that math together?"

"Sure," Matt answered. "You want a cookie before you go?"

"Sure," Tim said. "I'll go home and make sure it's okay with my mom if you come over. I'll call you here in a couple of minutes."

"Great," Matthew replied, watching his friend go out the door munching on a cookie.

"'Spence'? Would you care to explain?" his mother prompted.

"Yeah, well—" He started and stopped. "There are already two Matthews in sixth grade with me. It's been pretty confusing all year. One of them goes by 'Matt' and the other 'Matthew' so the teachers can keep them straight,'' he said. He paused for a moment and took a breath. ''The new semester started, and I'm ready to make a change. At school I'm going to be Spence. Is that all right?''

Grace nodded, not sure she could say anything. Matthew Spencer Mallory had just started the process of making a man out of the boy he would soon leave behind—a man who didn't want to be in the shadow of a father that no one, including himself, remembered too kindly. ''That's just fine. Do you want *us* to call you that, too?''

Matt reached for another cookie. Grace could see that he was trying to remain as casual as possible, not to show that it mattered to him one way or another. There would be no keeping important feelings out in the open for this boy. Not yet. ''If you would. I kind of like the way it sounds. Spence.''

''Then Spence it is,'' Carl said, ruffling his hair. ''Finish that cookie, Spence, then grab a broom. Somebody got crumbs all over the floor, here.''

They grinned at each other at that one, and Grace's heart soared. Somehow their exchange of looks felt like a conspiracy to her, a male bonding in which she played little part. Matt—no, Spence now—hadn't ever had that with a man before. Even though it meant she was letting go of him a little, seeing it happen felt wonderful.

"Do you need anything for supper?" Carl asked, watching the boy go to the storeroom for the broom.

"I could use a couple more potatoes," Grace said. "That is, if you two will want supper after all those cookies."

Carl's look of scorn made her burst out laughing. That stopped him in his tracks. "You laughed."

"I've never had someone speak a whole sentence to me before, just by quirking his eyebrow," Grace said, still stifling the last of her laughter.

"So, then, what did I say?" Carl challenged.

"You said, 'As if half-a-dozen measly cookies would keep me from supper, woman.'" Grace's mouth felt dry as he came closer to her.

"You're good at that. That is exactly what I said." He tipped her chin up to him, and Grace didn't resist the movement. "Even the 'woman' part, Grace. You are, you know, a woman. And I've noticed. Quite often."

Carl seemed oblivious to the large plate-glass window not ten feet away from them. For him there were no voices of children coming from the storeroom. So, for a moment, Grace entered his world and let him tip her chin higher; let his face come lower to hers until their lips met.

His kiss held the comfort of childhood—until she remembered her unhappy marriage, and tears sprang up in her eyes. Grace put both hands on his broad chest and pushed until the contact between them broke.

His eyes darkened with concern as he looked down at her. "What was I thinking?" he murmured. "I'm sorry. So sorry."

"So am I," Grace said, willing her voice not to break. "It won't happen again." She called for Maria, and half-blindly she wrapped the child in her scarf and quickly ushered her out the door. The wind tugged at the edges of Grace's sweater, reminding her of the ice she should be wrapping around her heart to keep herself safe.

What on earth have you done? Carl stood in the middle of the store, stunned. Grace's laughter had been so delightful and so unexpected. Laughter transformed her from the serious, guarded creature he'd seen since coming up to her porch so many weeks before. Instead, when she laughed she seemed little more than a girl, her cares fallen away and a new animation in her delicate features.

Then he'd gone and ruined the moment by kissing her. He'd wanted to for so long he hadn't been able to resist the urge.

He should have. Now everything felt all wrong. Grace had whisked out of the store more guarded than she'd been since Christmas. Until he'd looked deep into her eyes, when she'd pushed him away, Carl would have said it had been worth it.

She'd been so alive in his arms. Then, in a heartbeat, she'd turned into a small creature trapped and resisting him. The look on her face had been one of sheer panic. What had possessed him to force his attentions on her? He felt as if he'd vastly overstepped his bounds, and Grace probably felt that way about him, too. All because of one beautiful laugh.

Running a hand through his hair in frustration, Carl looked out the window to where Grace hurried Maria away. One beautiful, liquid laugh of pure joy. After the stunt he'd just pulled, it would be a long time, Carl knew, before he'd hear that sound again.

Chapter Eleven

It was two days before Carl got a civil word out of the woman, and three before she came near him. Even then, Carl felt that things with Grace were strange and stilted. If he'd known one kiss was going to cause that much trouble, he would have restrained himself. It drove him nearly mad to see her hangdog expression as she went about her precious duties. Why had he hired her as a housekeeper, anyway? Certainly not because he wanted a spotless house and food on the table at every opportunity. He wanted her company and that of her children, but once he'd kissed Grace Mallory, he got precious little of either for a long time.

At least the children still talked to him. The boy especially. Spence was blossoming in his new environment. When he'd first started working in the store, Carl had wished he'd smile at him once in a while. As they'd gone about their job together, the boy's silence and dogged persistence with every new task had surprised him. Spence had been all business. Now the boy had gotten to the point where he socialized with most of the customers who came into the store while he hung out there after school.

When Spence and Carl came home from work together, Maria waited at the back door, ready to tell him what they'd done all day and how she'd spent her time. Neither she nor the boy seemed to notice their mother's new reticence.

With so much free time on his hands, Carl could concentrate on finding Bill. It surprised him, though, that he couldn't work up any enthusiasm for the task.

It wasn't that he didn't want to find the young man. Kayla drooped around town like a wet mop. Every day after school she'd come into the store and ask if he'd had any word of Bill. She hadn't gotten a letter or a postcard or even a phone call. The girl was really beginning to worry. That alone should have gotten Carl going on the search.

He knew that once he started really looking for Bill, he'd probably locate him within a couple of days. That was the easy part. What he'd find once he tracked Bill down was what worried Carl. What if Bill had wanted to get away from Kayla and his very ordinary life in Redwing? Carl might not like Kayla all that well, but he didn't want to be the one to break her heart.

If Carl was honest with himself, there was another reason he was reluctant to find Bill. Once he located Bill, he'd have to keep his promise to find Jo Sparks. And Carl knew that as soon as he found Jo, he'd lose Grace and the kids.

He didn't doubt for a moment that when Grace knew where her aunt was, she would go to her. Staying here, keeping house for all of them and putting in a few hours a week in the store wouldn't be an option once Grace had real family. But then Carl would lose the only illusion of family he'd had in years.

He mulled all this over while he made half-hearted searches for Bill on the Internet. The easiest things didn't turn up any leads. The kid didn't have any credit cards in his own name that he could trace a payment schedule on. And no Bill, Billy, William, or even W. Parker had gotten a new listing with the phone company within the last thirty days anyplace in Missouri. It was disheartening.

Carl tried to reason and rationalize with himself. What would *he* do if he decided at nineteen that he was madly in love, that Redwing didn't hold any future worth talking about, and that he had to go make something of himself, right away? Bill was bright, but no rocket scientist. And three semesters of community college didn't lead to any jobs that were challenging. Not legal ones, anyway.

The kid was over eighteen, so legally he could sign himself up for just about anything. That included just about every branch of the armed forces, which was Carl's next place to check out. He knew the recruiters in Cape Girardeau and St. Louis didn't *have* to tell him anything. Still, they'd helped him out before when they could, so he spent one evening sending all of them E-mail. If nothing else, he reasoned, he'd have something to tell Kayla.

For the first time in a while, Carl regretted turning down the post office and the department of motor vehicles when they'd wanted him to run an office out of the store. Either one of them could have provided good solid leads for him, even if those weren't strictly legal. It was better this way, he told himself. Even to find Bill Parker, he wasn't ready to do anything of questionable legality.

The time in the evenings spent on the search meant that Carl was falling behind on ordering, invoices, and general bookkeeping for the store. He thought about asking Grace to man the counter for a couple of days so that he could catch up, but he couldn't do it.

No. Better to write and search the Internet in the silent parlor at night than suffer through a whole day of Grace's scent tantalizing him, Grace's warm body there at arm's length while her mind could have been a continent away. Just contemplating such a day drove him back to his computer screen every night.

Bill's mother wouldn't talk to him. At first she didn't know where he was; then later, when Carl was sure she did, she was upset with Kayla for driving her boy away to do whatever he'd done. When Carl couldn't get an answer out of her, he was pretty sure that Bill had gone into the service. If he'd taken a job in a larger city and leased an apartment there, Bill still could have come home to visit on his days off. Nope, his mother's aggravation spelled "basic training" to Carl.

He redoubled his efforts with the recruiters at night. Finally the army guy in Cape Girardeau gave him the response he'd been looking for. Carl didn't tell anybody he'd hit pay dirt. No sense getting Kayla's hopes up too soon. There was always the chance that Bill had joined the army to get away from Redwing *and* Kayla. If that was the case, Carl would find a way to break it to her as gently as possible—but only after he'd talked to Bill and his mother.

"Nine weeks," Bill's mother told him, her lips pressed tightly shut. "And four of them still to go.

Of course I told him he had to use his phone calls home to talk to me, not that little—"

"Now hold on, Mrs. Parker," Carl interrupted, trying to head something ugly off at the pass. "By the army's definition, Bill's a grown man. If he wanted to join up, you can't blame it on Kayla."

"I most certainly can." Janet Parker looked older than the nearly fifty Carl knew she was. Of course, life in a little town like Redwing, with nobody but your nineteen-year-old son to depend on, couldn't be easy. "I can blame her plenty. If it wasn't for wanting to 'be somebody' for that girl, Bill would have stayed right here and finished school, kept his part-time job at the gas station out on the highway and done just fine."

"He might have done all that—" Carl tried to stay calm "—but would he have done just fine? You've lived here for most of your life, Janet. What was the boy going to do once he finished school? Go to work at the auto-parts plant in Cape? Stayed pumping gas? Aren't you glad Bill wanted more than that?"

The lines in Janet's thin face softened. "I am glad he wants more. Guess I just miss him, is all."

"When's graduation from basic at Fort Leonard Wood?" Carl knew the answer already, but thought this might be the chance for some bridge building.

"Second weekend in April." Janet's expression was sour. "But that old truck wouldn't make it there without an overhaul. And I don't have anybody to do it anymore, do I?"

"No, I guess you don't. But if you could see your way clear to making a little deal with me, I think we can get you to that graduation."

Janet's pale, tired eyes narrowed. "Will *she* be going too, if we make this deal?"

Carl sighed. "Yes, Kayla will be going, too. But you'd better get used to saying her name, Janet. Sounds like if Bill has his way, you're going to get to know her real well eventually. Maybe even like one of the family."

Janet huffed out a breath, making her nostrils flare. To Carl she looked more like a Missouri mule than ever, until she finally smiled. "Oh, all right. I'll even make up with her—I mean Kayla— if it means seeing my boy graduate. What do you propose, Carl?"

"Lousy groundhog." Grace was tempted to shake her fist at the nonexistent animal. February had started this gray and dank thanks to him, and was ending the same way. She was ready for spring now. Why was it so long in coming? Grace peered through the darkness at the kitchen window, wishing the dark didn't come so early in the evening. Wishing that Carl was home from his mysterious errand. It had to be important for him to go someplace for the whole day, leaving her to mind the store, but he hadn't said much about where he'd be.

Of course, he hadn't said much to her in the last month, nor had she said much to him. She'd felt frozen since he'd kissed her, willing her feelings into ice so that she could stay under the same roof with him without losing her mind.

She'd wondered how she could face Carl after the kiss and had tried to hide her feelings. But even in her dismay over kissing Carl in broad daylight and showing him just how deeply it affected her, Grace didn't want to forget that kiss. She couldn't repeat it, but she wasn't anywhere near ready to forget it.

If only he'd come down to breakfast the next morning smiling and whistling like before. Then she might have thawed some. Might have spoken more, loosened her hair from the tight knot she knew he despised. Might have made an effort to speak with him to pass the time of day while she cooked his breakfast or served his supper.

Instead, he had been as grim as she had felt herself that morning, and Grace found herself building up an extra shell of ice around herself that hadn't thawed yet. Or at least it hadn't thawed all the way. She couldn't be in the same house with the man—cooking for him every day and doing his laundry, sitting in his parlor at night while he messed with that computer and she helped Spence study or read to Maria—without warming a little.

Still, drawing away from Carl for a while had been a good thing, she decided. She felt changes inside herself, changes she couldn't deny anymore. The quiet time over the last few weeks also meant that he hadn't had to bear the brunt of her anger.

Anger had come out of nowhere following that January kiss and swamped her like river waves over a child's homemade boat. Who did Carl think he was to just kiss her like that in public in the store? And even more troubling, why hadn't any man's kiss ever felt like that before? Could it be possible, Grace asked herself over and over during those long winter weeks, that she hadn't ever really known love between a man and a woman the way it was meant to be?

At first, asking such a question only made her anger and frustration rise. She fought the feelings by plunging herself into hard, physical work every day. The house shone. Every sheet, towel, blanket and tablecloth got ironed, mended and put away in top condition. She found dishes and knickknacks Carl didn't know he had. She straightened closets, beat rugs when the weather cleared enough to do it, and went to bed each night so tired she could barely walk up the stairs.

The physical tiredness didn't keep her from lying awake, staring at the ceiling. She must have remembered every nuance of that one kiss fifty times. Folding each clean shirt reminded her of how Carl smelled and felt wearing it. Just sitting next to him at the dinner table mesmerized her as she watched his mouth move.

She couldn't live this way much longer. Cleaning the house was a poor substitute for talking to Carl. Cooking meals didn't make her want to touch him any less. Something had to change soon, Grace told herself, as she looked out the window into the dark. She was ready for spring. And ready, definitely, for change.

Change came in the door with Carl that dark late February night. Grace heard the truck in the yard, the slam of doors. He messed with something outside until she thought she'd scream. Finally he was on the porch, stomping mud off his boots, using the iron scraper outside the door for what seemed like an interminable time.

Suddenly she couldn't keep her silence, her detachment.

"Well? Where have you been all day? What did you find out? Get those boots off and have some coffee and tell me all about it," she said, as if they hadn't been strangers to each other lately.

Carl looked slightly perplexed, but not totally confused. First he just stood there for a while, his hand on the doorknob. "You're letting in all the cold air,'' Grace informed him, as if he didn't know that.

He looked outside and broke into a grin. ''Guess I am. And we can't have that.'' He stuck his head out the door and whistled. Four came bounding in after him, dancing in his excitement to see Grace.

''Yes, and I missed you, too,'' she said, trying not to laugh while large, feather-furred paws climbed nearly to her shoulders and the dog planted a sloppy cold kiss halfway between her chin and cheek.

She pushed him off, gently. ''Oh, get down. You're not a long-lost orphan. Besides, you're probably muddy.''

Carl tried to sound indignant instead of indulgent and failed. ''You have that dog spoiled rotten.''

He took off his boots and clumped over to the table stocking-footed. ''You have me spoiled rotten, too, Grace. I didn't realize how good I had it around here with you until I left for a day.''

Grace's heart thudded so hard she nearly dropped the coffeepot. ''Now what can you mean by that?''

''What I can, and do, mean by that is I ate a purely awful lunch in Cape Girardeau, at a table not half so convivial as mine usually is even when you don't talk.''

''Cape Girardeau? What on earth were you doing there? And what have you been doing since lunchtime?'' She couldn't help it. This time her shaking hand betrayed her and coffee slopped over the rim of the cup as she poured. ''I'll clean that up,'' she said, surprised by the fear that swamped her—fear that had no purpose any longer, but still haunted her when she made what for Matt had been unforgivable mistakes, like spilling the coffee.

''No problem.'' Carl didn't even seem to notice the puddle under his cup. ''Do we have cream?''

''Coming right up.'' She whisked away the spilled coffee, put the wet rag on the sink top and went for the milk in the refrigerator. She kept her shaking hands under control as she set the jug on the table, and when Carl patted the chair next to him, she pushed away her usual protestations and sat.

''So tell me all about it,'' she said, bubbling with an excitement she could see mirrored in Carl's tired eyes. ''You found Bill?''

''I found Bill. And in early April we're going to take a trip across the state to see him.'' She listened as he spun the tale of where his search had led, and what he'd done even that day. The dog took advantage of her rapt attention to Carl and nosed his way under her hand, insinuating himself under the table to do so, even though they both knew he wasn't supposed to be there.

Carl was telling her about his conversation with Janet before she realized she was stroking silky ears and there was a large, thumping tail beating time to his words. "All right. Just this once. But beg under the table while we eat and you'll be in disgrace." The large paw that stroked her knee for a moment seemed a promise that Four would be a gentleman.

Carl's coffee cup was empty and his hands were on the table. "How about me, Grace? Am I still in disgrace? Or have I finally redeemed myself by finding the boy?"

He looked so serious, waiting for her answer. Grace couldn't help but get up—so quickly that her chair tipped over. In an instant she was in his arms. It felt so good. She felt so welcome to be there, savoring the warmth of him, the crispness of his hair against her cheek.

"Oh, Carl. You were never in disgrace. It was me. I know I made such a fool of myself when you kissed me. I couldn't let that happen again."

His eyes were bright as he drew her down closer into his embrace. "Well, if you couldn't let that happen again you should have stayed over in that chair, because I sure want to kiss you again."

His words should have stopped her, should have chilled her blood and sent her racing to safety across the room. But instead she came closer, and they kissed.

This kiss was a welcome back. Back to where she should have been while she'd been berating herself instead.

"So I'm forgiven?" he asked.

"Nothing to forgive."

"I think there was. I know I came on too strong, too quick before. I'll take things slower now, I promise." He looked so boyishly earnest that laughter bubbled up in Grace again. He was so different from any man she'd ever known before. So delightful in all his moods, from somber to happy.

"You do that, then. And you'll start looking for Aunt Jo?"

A look flickered over his face, and then was gone. Grace wasn't sure what she'd seen. Was it doubt, or guilt, or something else equally puzzling? It came and went so quickly, she wasn't sure.

"We'll find Jo," Carl said as he got up. "But for now I am nearly dead on my feet. And I've got to go up to bed."

Grace didn't argue, even though she yearned to have him stay. Better he left than they both had to struggle with the feelings one more kiss had lit in them.

Since she couldn't do anything about the warmth Carl had started in her, she did more practical things instead. She made sure the milk was put away, that the coffeepot was empty and the lights out. Then she went to bed and for a change she fell asleep quickly, still staring at the ceiling but now tracing her lips with one bemused finger, and fighting giggles in the dark so as not to disturb Maria.

Chapter Twelve

Spring weather hadn't arrived, but it was spring in Grace's heart. The crocuses were blooming amid drifts of late snow. The wind was still as raw and wet as ever, and yet Grace expected to be able to go out in shirtsleeves and gather heaps of daffodils. Surely if she felt this way inside, it must be spring outside the front door, too.

Her good humor seemed to be catching. Carl went off to the store each morning, whistling as loud as Spence. Sometimes, coming home, Grace caught them racing. She suspected that Carl had to rein himself in quite a bit to let the boy win.

During the first week in March, Kayla came bubbling over to the house twice. She had to be almost physically restrained from hugging Carl and the dog, neither of whom wanted the attention.

First there had been a letter from Bill and then on Sunday night, a phone call.

"He loves me." She danced around the room, not able to sit still. "He's almost finished with basic training and then he goes to school at Fort Bragg in South Carolina. Then he'll be a specialist, and he'll get leave. When he comes back I think he's going to talk to Dad about getting married. Can you believe it?"

Grace couldn't answer right away. For once, Grace blessed Carl for not moving into town next to the store. Most of the time she felt a little isolated out on the edge of things, but when Kayla had big news like this, it was worthwhile to be the first to hear their awkward plans.

They were so achingly young. Grace wanted to give them all kinds of cautions. Carl just looked uncomfortable avoiding Kayla's dance around the kitchen while he drank his coffee. Grace wondered if it was Kayla's discovery of her adulthood that made Carl look that antsy, or just worry that he'd drop the cup.

It wasn't long before the half-grown cat batting at her moving shoestrings gave Kayla the giggles and she sat down. Granted, it was on the floor with the cat, but things were calmer that way. The children ate the cookies Grace was taking out of the oven, and Four made little snorts and moans in the doorway for being excluded from what he perceived as a grand party.

Carl seemed relieved when Kayla headed back to Larry's, the kitchen cleared out, and left them alone cleaning up. "Kayla's very happy," Grace said, rinsing a cup.

"I guess." He sounded tentative.

"I know they don't know what they're getting themselves into, but nobody could tell them that. Especially not a girl as young as Kayla."

"No, probably not." Carl dried the cup with exaggerated concern. "But do you think this will all work out?"

"As well as marriage ever works out," Grace said, trying to sound optimistic. "They seem to love each other. That's a good start."

"Wouldn't it be a better start if he had some money? And she had a little more age on her, and some common sense?"

Grace looked into Carl's face. Usually he kept his emotions to himself, but this time he seemed to have revealed a genuine concern for the young couple. "Kayla's got plenty of sense. I know she looks flighty to you, but that's just because you're not used to giggly girls. And Bill's got plenty of money. You don't need much, starting out."

"If you say so. I'd want more than that to offer a woman. As far as that goes, I'd want more than I have right now to offer a woman." He'd put down the next cup, still swathed in a towel, and was facing her now.

"I mean, marriage ought to start out right. A good house, a steady job—all that is fine. But the people need to be worthwhile, too, don't they?"

He was troubled in a way that Grace hadn't seen in him before. "What are you saying, Carl? I don't think you're talking about Bill and Kayla anymore."

"I'm not. Not just about them, anyway. I guess they'll get by just fine. He'll probably have to put up with a few burned dinners and they'll fight some if his mama comes to live with them, I expect, but they'll get along fine. But Grace, who would ever want me?"

"I would." The words came out so quickly, they surprised her as much as they seemed to surprise Carl. "I would, Carl." She repeated them, just to taste their delicate sweetness on her tongue.

"Would you? There are things you don't know about me. Things that aren't too pleasant. I'm not as good as you think I am, Grace. And there're things most men bring to a marriage that I can't bring."

"Such as?" As long as he was in a talkative mood, Grace thought, might as well get everything out in the open. After being married to Matt Mallory for ten years, she wouldn't start again with that many surprises.

"I have no family. Few friends. No real connections at all. Even the family that's not there anymore isn't one to claim. I never thought that would be fair. To a woman, I mean, and to children." There were little white tracings of the faint lines around his mouth. His admission had cost him dear, and Grace wanted to repay him for the effort he'd expended.

She wiped her hands quickly on her apron. No sense spattering him with dishwater. Smoothing the lines from around his tense mouth, she held his face between her hands. "Is that supposed to matter to me?"

He looked surprised. "You mean you wouldn't care? About not having anybody? You want to find Jo so bad, I figured family would be doubly important to you."

"There're more important things that I worry about," Grace admitted. "I've got two fine children in your parlor. Could you care for another man's child? Or will you just resent them and where they came from?"

His head dipped, and roughly, he kissed her palm. His action told her so much before he even spoke. "I'd already take anybody apart who tried to hurt those two. I can't help it, Grace. I don't care who planted the seed. I'd like to help the tree grow."

There was a fierce joy building in Grace that

threatened to burst out in tears. "It's too soon," she murmured, feeling frustrated and happy at the same time. "I'm not ready for this. Besides, the whole town would say scandalous things. Can you wait?"

"I can wait. But not for long, Grace. And not patiently. I'm not a patient man, no matter what people are going to say."

"I don't much care, either," Grace admitted. "They've been talking about me for the whole time I've lived here, I expect. What's to matter if they have something new to talk about now? But let's wait a little while more."

"If that's what you want." He released her hand from its trap and stared into her eyes, making her shiver.

"It's what I need. For now."

"For now," Carl echoed, his voice taut with unspoken emotion. The water Grace put her hands back into had grown cold. With a shiver that had little to do with the cold water, she hurried to freshen up the dishwater.

It was Kayla who changed Grace's mind about waiting. Kayla in her innocence, who never knew what she'd said. Despite what she'd told Carl, Grace did have a few questions about Kayla's ability to be a good wife to Bill. She was still so young and dreamy that Grace wondered if she'd get anything done the first few months of marriage, or just play house a little. Perhaps Bill wouldn't mind if he got to play, too, Grace told herself.

Thinking of them "playing house" put a smile on her face the next time Kayla came over for housekeeping lessons and cooking help. She did seem a little more serious as the morning wore on. As they worked in the kitchen together there seemed to be a question on the tip of Kayla's kittenish pink tongue. Grace wondered how to get her to ask it without embarrassing the girl—sure that it had nothing to do with their activities in the kitchen.

The cuckoo clock in the parlor had chirped eleven before Grace found a way to prod the girl into speech. "So what does your dad think about all this?" Grace tried to sound casual.

"He's okay with it, I guess. He wasn't at first, but he is now. Bill's looking at when he will get another furlough once he's posted to his first assignment. Bill says he doesn't believe in long engagements, and Dad says we'd better not, anyway," Kayla said, still concentrating on the checkbook balance in front of her.

"Oh? Did he have a reason?" Perhaps this was the source of her questions. The checkbook was hopeless as far as Grace could tell. They were going to have a long talk later about entering things *when* the check was written. Entries marked "Stuff" and "About $20" just didn't cut it for her.

"I thought we could wait for a while, and maybe I could go up to Fort Bragg and help Bill look for a house. He wants to go off base to live. And I expect his mother will come, too. But Dad said no. He said something about all the money Bill would be spending to furnish a house and if I wasn't careful maybe he'd want to take it out in trade, like you and Mr. Brenner."

Kayla looked shocked then, realizing whom she was talking to and what she'd just said. Grace didn't answer at first. With shaking hands she directed Kayla on how to at least halfway balance the checkbook mess.

"Dad didn't mean…" Kayla started.

"I know, Kayla." Grace did know exactly what Larry had meant, but she wasn't going to say that in front of the girl. She might have a terse discussion with Larry later, but she wouldn't take her anger out on Kayla. "I expect he just meant it wouldn't look too good, an unmarried girl like you in a big town like that with Bill, even with his mother along. And it is expensive to furnish a house, Kayla."

"Do you really owe Carl money?"

"Not anymore. He's paying me a salary for keeping house for him. The first few weeks I worked for what I owed him, mainly for Matt's

escapades in town.'' Grace struggled to keep her
voice as even as the column of figures growing in
the checkbook. It was no mean feat. She could always pretend the column of red ink was Larry
Trent and the rest of the sanctimonious old men in
town. Leave it to them to figure that Carl had found
an arrangement that didn't include money to pay
his housekeeper.

Grace wasn't about to tell Kayla how much Carl
insisted on paying her. Or that he wouldn't take
anything back for board for her and the children.
Fortunately Kayla didn't ask any more questions—
not about Carl and Grace's situation, anyway. By
the time the checkbook was finally balanced,
Grace's hands had stopped shaking. And Kayla
wanted to know how to starch and iron lace curtains, as if she and Bill could afford any.

Tactfully refraining from pointing out that fact,
Grace took the bank statement Kayla had brought
over out of its envelope and began to go over it
with her so the checkbook mess wouldn't happen
again. And all the while most of her mind was
elsewhere, wondering how she would break the
news to Carl that the whole town was besmirching
their good name. *His* good name, probably. Grace
didn't think she had much of a good name with
anybody in Redwing—a situation that wouldn't
change unless she married Carl Brenner, and
quickly.

* * *

"It just doesn't look right," Larry said. "She's a healthy young woman and you're not exactly some ailing old codger. Having a housekeeper live in at your age is just leading to talk."

"Well, that's all it's leading to. Talk. Don't you people have anything better to do at town-council meetings than run down honest people?" Carl couldn't keep the aggravation out of his voice. Maybe he'd feel differently about things if he were actually doing what Larry was hinting at. At least then, he'd probably have a healthy dose of guilt about his situation instead of the frustration that made Larry's pronouncement even harder to take.

"Look, Carl, I really appreciate what you've done for me. And I've tried to tell the rest of them to hold off on saying anything. I mean, the woman's still a widow and all. I know she needs someplace to live and it's just Christian charity on your part that makes you give her a home."

"No, Larry, it's a sight more than Christian charity." Carl stayed still and just hollered. He could feel his neck getting redder, starting first at the level of his collar, then rising slowly up to his hairline.

"I am not giving Grace Mallory a home out of charity, Christian or otherwise. She's gotten that house cleaner than it's ever been since I've lived in it. Spence is as good a helper around the store as anybody I've hired in five years, and he's not even eleven yet. And she's a fine woman who I intend to make my wife. Couldn't you let me do it in my own time?''

''I would on my own.'' Larry's tone had become a definite whine now. ''But that girl of mine is going in and out of your house all the time. She's probably got enough ideas about how things are supposed to go with that Parker kid already. All she needs to see is the two of you—''

That was it. Carl's fist came down on the counter that separated the two of them with a violence that rattled the light fixtures. ''What on earth do you think she's seeing, Larry? The woman is my housekeeper.''

''Try telling that to the women. I don't have a wife at home to contend with, but the other three do. And they're all convinced that two young, healthy people under the same roof with nobody for company but two little kids are bound to get into trouble. And they want it stopped.''

''Great. So the town biddies have decided that I can either throw out the best housekeeper I've ever had, or ask her to marry me. Which, this close to her moving in, will probably make her so mad at me she'll leave.''

Larry looked a little wan. ''I guess that's about the size of it. I didn't think of it your way before I came over here, Carl. And if I had, maybe I would have tried harder to talk to the rest of them about this. But Fred says he hasn't had any peace for weeks at home, and Pete has that snippy little daughter who's going to school with Spence. I wanted to say something to you before that kid gets it into her head to spread nasty rumors she's heard from her mother.''

Carl's heart sank. "I think you're too late for that one. Thanks for warning me, at least." He leaned on the counter, trying to ease the tension out of his taut shoulders and back. It would have felt so much better just to punch Larry and get it over with. But it wouldn't solve his problems, no matter how good it would make him feel. Better to talk it out today. "I'll speak to Grace. And Spence. And we'll find some way to shut up the gossips. But this better not foul up my chances of marrying this woman later.''

Larry actually blanched. "I keep trying to tell you it's not my fault, Carl. Go blame the rest of them.''

"Oh, no, Larry," Carl growled. "You're the mayor. You're in charge. I'm holding you responsible if this falls apart because of the 'good women' of Redwing and their objections.''

The mayor left quickly after that. For his own part, Carl just lowered himself to his high stool and traced patterns on the scarred surface of the countertop before him, mulling over how to break the news to Grace.

The talk with Grace was going to be rough. But at least Carl had an idea of what to say. He figured there would be a lot of recriminations from the proud woman in his kitchen. She wasn't going to take kindly to the thought of marrying him just because a flock of old hens was clucking about the two of them.

Worse would be the talk he was going to have with Spencer. He had no idea how to begin that one—especially when he remembered the shiner the boy had come in with the day before. Spence had glossed over the bruise high on his cheekbone, claiming it was due to some roughhousing at lunchtime. Now, Carl had a suspicion it was part of something else altogether.

All too soon the bell over the door jingled to herald the boy's arrival. He wasn't bouncing into the place as usual, and Carl remembered that he'd walked like this the day before, too. Stiff-legged and slow, as if he had to make himself come in, instead of with his normal enthusiasm.

Carl let him go into the back room to put away his things. Then he pulled out the little sign to close the shop; he had more important business to tend to for a while. Mounting the sign on the door, Carl locked it and went back to face the boy.

It wouldn't be easy. He didn't want to offend the kid, not now. The last thing Grace's son probably wanted was somebody to take the place of a father he hadn't been all that fond of, judging by what he *hadn't* said.

The boy looked up in surprise as Carl entered the back room. "I made sure it's just the two of us for a few minutes, Spence. Man to man. And I think I know how you got that shiner. Why don't you tell me about it."

Kids could be so ugly, Carl thought to himself. He'd willed himself not to wince while the boy poured out his story about Pete's daughter and her comment. "And I couldn't hit her. She's a girl. Mom would have my hide if I ever hit a girl. And her brother's in the eighth grade."

"But you hit him anyway," Carl said, knowing the answer from the scrapes on the boy's knuckles that he'd missed seeing the day before.

Spence nodded. "And got pounded. And then got in trouble with the pastor when he picked us up for car pool, for fighting at school. He wanted to talk to Mom, but once the kids told him what the fight was all about, he changed his mind about that. At least none of the teachers saw it."

"You'd be in worse trouble, then."

Spence nodded. "Yeah, suspended. But so would Jessica's big brother." The last was delivered with a grim satisfaction that belied a spirit older than his ten years, and far more bitter than Carl wanted any ten-year-old to be.

"You know they're not right."

"Sure. But there's no way I'm going to convince them of that. Anything I say or do is just going to make it all worse."

He looked so dejected, Carl couldn't resist putting a hand on his narrow shoulder. "What would you say if your mother and I got married? Not right away. And not to shut up those old hens in town."

Straightening, the boy looked startled. "Would that make me a Brenner? Because—"

"No, it would only make your mother a Brenner. If she'd even have me. You'd stay a Mallory for as long as you wanted to." Carl expected to see relief on the boy's face, and felt confused when his expression seemed to mirror more disappointment than solace.

"So you don't want us."

The flat statement delivered with such matter-of-factness drove Carl to his knees, both physically and mentally. "Never say that. It isn't true. I just figured you had a father already, and I don't want to try and take his place."

"You've already done more than take his place. I'm going to school. Nobody makes Mom cry and worry. I've stopped having nightmares." There were tears in the boy's eyes. "I just figured it was too good to last."

"It's not good *enough*, Spence. There's so much more I'd like to do for all three of you. And it would be a package deal, boy. I wouldn't marry your mother without figuring that all three of you came together.'' He hugged the boy fiercely for a moment.

"I'll never intentionally hurt her. Or you or Maria, either. I had too much of that as a kid and I know what it feels like. You'll always have a roof over your head and a real family. As much education as I can afford to give you both. And if you want to take my name, I'd be proud. But I don't feel like it's much of a name."

Carl stood and backed off, giving the boy time to compose himself. "If you want to marry Mom, I'd like that. A lot. And we'll see about the name business. I'm still getting used to being Spence Mallory."

"Spence Brenner sounds kinda funny, doesn't it?" Carl said, trying it out on his tongue. The boy nodded solemnly. "Well, we'll work on it. Before that, we've got something bigger to work on. How am I going to convince your mom that she ought to marry me?"

Spence shrugged. "Don't look at me. I can't even get her to let me stay up half an hour later on school nights." The tension in Carl exploded in laughter at the boy's blunt statement. He was right. This was a problem Carl was going to have to solve for himself. Maybe going over to Naomi's for pie with the boy would give him an idea or two. At least they'd both be less hungry. He clapped his arm around Spencer's shoulder, and they went out to tend to business.

Chapter Thirteen

All the way home, Carl rehearsed different speeches in his head. None of them sounded right. Reasons for getting married should be romantic, shouldn't they? His real reasons were romantic. Or at least, better than "Larry and the town council think we're living in sin." He couldn't very well tell her that.

He couldn't tell her the way he felt right away either. That he could hardly stand being next to her so much of the day without touching her. That wanting her kept him awake nights and made him mess up the bookkeeping in the store. If this burning kept on much longer without relief he was going to go broke from his own mistakes. And hadn't Saint Paul said that it was better to marry than to burn? Grace probably wasn't going to see it Saint Paul's way.

When he got home, the first few minutes of bedlam didn't give him any room for a serious discussion. Maria, the cat and Four all tangled in a happy melee around him as soon as he got in the door. It did his heart good to see the little girl strong and boisterous. She had looked pretty sick for a while, but Tom Conrad had recently pronounced her in perfect health. Still, he worried. Probably not the way her mother did, but it gave him a taste of what parenthood must be like.

He swung her around, delighting in her hair smelling faintly of baby shampoo and her delicious chuckles at being tossed in the air. "Don't throw her too high," her mother cautioned. "She had a cookie while we waited for you two to get home. I don't want it to come back."

"Yes, ma'am," Carl said in mock contrition, swinging the child back to the ground. Then it was the dog's turn for a little wrestling.

"Now go wash your hands. I don't want you sitting down to supper with dog hair all over you," Grace chided. Carl looked at her, wondering at the sharpness of her tone. Her face was pale, looking pinched in a way he hadn't seen it since just after Christmas. With a rush of anger, he wondered if Larry had come and talked to her, too. If he had, Carl resolved to boot him into the next county.

"Any visitors today?" He tried to keep his tone casual for the children. No sense in getting them upset ahead of time.

"Just Kayla," Grace said, which made him relax a little. Still, there was something wrong. His sense of that didn't dissipate any during supper, when Grace pushed around a bowl of stew without ever really eating any of it. She didn't even pretend to want any of the cherry pie she gave everybody else.

Grace seemed to want to talk to him alone as much as he wanted to talk to her. For a change she dispatched both children to the parlor after supper, insisting that it was Carl's turn to help her with the dishes. It was never Carl's turn to help with the dishes.

Still, nobody argued with her. Spence, who'd already finished his homework at the store, took Maria into the parlor to read to her, and even the dog trooped in after them. Carl figured there must be serious discussion afoot for the dog to sense it in the air and slink out. For a moment he wished he could join them.

"Are you sure Larry didn't come by here this afternoon?"

"Positive. I take it he came by the store," Grace said. Her expression told him what she thought of Larry's visit, even though she hadn't had one herself.

"He did. But Larry didn't sound like Larry. He

sounded like some meddling old busybody. He thinks we ought to get married. Or you ought to move out. According to him, it just doesn't look right, our being young and healthy and under the same roof."

"He's right—it's not his business. But he *is* right, Carl." Her voice was so soft, with an edge that betrayed a broken heart. "Kayla's been hearing things—not just from him but from other places, too. People are talking."

She silently scrubbed a couple more dishes, rinsed them in a pan of clear water and stacked them for Carl to dry. "Would you rather move out?" Carl finally asked, hating to voice his suspicions. He couldn't imagine Grace wanting to marry him. Not now, at least. They'd just started talking about maybe. Someday.

She put down the mug she was washing and looked straight at him. Her look of consternation made his heart soar. "Move out? I just moved in! But if that's what you think is best, I guess we could. Maybe…"

Carl's heart was pounding as fast as if he'd run all the way home from the store. He grabbed Grace before she could get any further on this train of thought. "No. Whoa, slow down, here. We're both making assumptions about what the other one wants to do. Let me start over."

Saying anything more was going to be so hard

while he held her. But there couldn't be any other way. If he let go, Grace would withdraw. She'd start packing those boxes, first mentally, and then for real. If that happened, he'd never get a chance to have any kind of life with her.

Carl took a deep breath and loosened his grip on her shoulders, so that it felt more like a caress than a restraint. "Okay, Grace, here goes. I'm not good at this kind of stuff, and this is a lousy situation, but I want to make the best of it. And stop wriggling." He tried to sound stern. It must have succeeded, because her brown eyes widened and she stood still in his arms. "I want you to marry me. I don't want you to move out, and I'm not happy with Larry and the town council for pushing us into this before you're ready.

"But at the same time I could kiss them all for doing it, because I don't know when I would have gotten up the courage to ask without a little push. Grace, I want you to marry me. And not because some old biddies in town are talking about us. I'll take care of you, and your kids, as long as I live. You'll never go hungry or without anything."

Her nose wrinkled. "You're right. That's the most unromantic proposal I've ever heard. But at least you're honest. You seem to be a fine man, Carl. Honest and a good provider. When I was seventeen, those weren't the reasons I thought I'd get married. But now, at twenty-eight with two kids, there are a whole lot of worse reasons.''

Her arms came up to join his embrace. Carl pulled her to him. ''Of course, if we get married now, it will just give them something else to talk about.''

''I know.'' Her words were a little muffled in his shirt front, but still sounded tart. ''I can either be labeled a brazen hussy for being your housekeeper and giving you the milk for free instead of making you buy the cow, or I can be labeled a brazen hussy for marrying you after only knowing you a couple of months.'' She pulled back from him, and Carl was delighted to see the glow of suppressed laughter in her eyes instead of tears. ''I think I'd rather be a *married* brazen hussy, if it's all right with you. Or at least an *engaged* one, so they'll stop talking.''

''It's just what I had in mind.'' And finally he bent down and kissed her, promising her all the protection he could give her within the circle of his arms.

''I do have one or two conditions.'' Here it came. The reasons she was looking up at him like this.

Carl sighed. ''Go ahead. Tell me what they are.''

''No great big rock. We'll go over to the discount store in Jackson and get a ring, and that will be it. And I'll marry you, Carl Brenner, when my Aunt Jo can give me away.''

Carl felt his heart plummet to his shoes. The first condition was easy. The second one felt impossible. Still, he couldn't let on to Grace that that was the way he felt. "Agreed." He could barely choke the word out and still smile, but he did it. It almost killed him, but he got it done.

Grace looked down at her finger, bemused. She was really engaged to Carl Brenner. It was amazing that a tiny circle of gold and a couple of diamond chips went so far toward shutting everybody up. At least the wedding planning and the finding Jo would carry them past Easter and right into spring. Somehow she couldn't face being married again in the same season they'd buried Matt. This marriage, when it happened, would have nothing of winter in it.

What she'd had with Matt had stopped feeling like a marriage long before it had ended, if it ever had been one. Looking at other couples in a new light, she wondered if theirs had ever been a marriage in the true sense of the word. It certainly had never felt the way to her, from the inside, that other marriages looked from the outside. Doc Conrad walked up to the cemetery with flowers or a card or something every Sunday. He didn't go to church, but he visited his wife's grave. Watching him from a distance, Grace suspected he still talked over the difficult times with her. She was surprised when she'd gone into the cemetery herself to see that Mrs. Conrad had died nearly ten years ago. And her husband still came every Sunday to pass the time.

Even Bill and Kayla seemed to be looking forward to marriage in a way that surprised Grace. Every other Saturday Bill used his one phone call to talk to Kayla, and the next week he called his mother. The women got friendly enough to trade information, so that nobody went without for very long. And everybody was looking forward to going to Bill's graduation.

Grace tried to view her own impending marriage in a practical way. She spent most of her time talking to Maria, preparing her for the somewhat-confusing changes that would take place in her life. Spence seemed to be handling it well. Grace suspected that he and Carl had come to some tacit agreement at the store, because he showed no surprise when Grace broached the subject to him.

The biggest changes—the ones she wasn't anywhere near ready to contemplate—were the domestic ones. Grace found herself going into Carl's room just to convince herself that she had actually agreed to marry this man and sleep here with him.

It was a nice room. Big windows let in plenty of air and sunshine. The bed itself looked huge, taking up the middle of the room on a bright rag rug. There would be plenty of space in it for the two of them never to run into each other, Grace suspected.

Even more surprising to her was that Carl had insisted that the two vacant bedrooms on the same floor of the house—long locked and echoing with emptiness—be fixed up for the children, including new bedspreads and curtains for each room. "You can make a day of it, go to the mall in Cape Girardeau with Kayla. You both need new clothes for the graduation anyway, don't you?"

"I suppose." Grace knew she'd sounded dubious. She hadn't given the subject much thought. Her everyday jeans wouldn't do, though, and even she was getting tired of her one good dress.

Kayla was more than happy to take the day off from school the following Monday for a shopping expedition.

"I should probably give you my purse, and Daddy's credit cards," Kayla teased as they walked into the mall. "You're supposed to keep me in line, remember?"

"That's only when we're spending money." As Grace looked around at all the stores, she felt like a teenager herself. It was a wonderful, heady feeling, and she intended to keep it for the entire day if she could.

They hit every department store in the mall, which wasn't hard since it only had three. Going through most of the ladies' specialty stores was fun, too, Grace discovered. Had she ever shopped like this with anyone else? Jo had never been a shopper, and Grace just figured she was missing the gene herself. But this was fun, even when she wasn't spending much.

They had lunch at the food court to fortify themselves for the shopping ahead. Grace hadn't eaten a meal in a restaurant without the kids in years. Here, among the ladies who 'lunched,' she felt almost elegant. So elegant that she insisted on treating Kayla to the meal, including ice cream for dessert. "Can you afford that?" Kayla asked, continuing her role of shepherding Grace around.

"Of course. I'm a woman of means, remember?" It was true, after a fashion. Carl had insisted on paying her in cash for the past month, and was adamant that he wanted her to spend her wages on herself and the children.

Most of the money she'd already spent in Carl's store, making sure that Spence had a coat that fit and Maria a cute new outfit for school. But standing in the mall now, Grace felt reluctant to spend the remainder. It was the first time in years she'd had this much cash in hand. "I feel strange spending this much money on myself," she said to Kayla.

"But you're getting married!" Kayla exclaimed. "I've got that much to spend on myself, too. That's why we're here, remember? I can't spend anything knowing you're holding back, Mrs. Mallory. It would make me feel too awful."

Grace looked at the girl. It *would* make her feel bad. Under her flighty exterior, Kayla had a soft heart that went out to anything and anybody, from orphaned baby birds on up. There was no sense in confessing all her worries to someone so excited about life.

Still, the girlishness that had been building in Grace all day bubbled to the surface in giggles. She was twenty-eight years old and she'd never had a chance to be a carefree girl like Kayla. Her first wedding had been a hurried affair to a dour man. And yet she was still young, had her health and a fine man ready to marry her. And money in her pocket.

"But I'm supposed to be the good influence on you here," Grace said, dismayed.

Kayla made a face. "The last thing I want today is a good influence, Mrs. Mallory."

"Then let's get to it, Kayla," she replied.

The trip to Fort Leonard Wood for Bill's graduation started off uncomfortably. Carl silently cursed himself for not having considered seating arrangements in the truck. He should have realized that Janet Parker wouldn't want to sit next to Kayla in the back seat for so long. So it ended with Kayla and Grace in the back, and him up front with Janet.

Carl was surprised they made the whole three-hour trip without Grace wanting to call home. He knew that the kids would be fine with Barb and Hal Peterson, and that they'd remember to look in on the animals often. But he was thankful that Grace had decided everything was all right that way too.

Nor did their stop for coffee in a roadside fast-food outlet loosen anybody up much. Carl tried to make small talk, most of which fell flat. He decided things had to get better once they got to Bill's graduation.

When they all stood in line after the ceremonies, Carl watched Grace. She was quiet, even had her eyes closed some. "What are you thinking?" he asked softly. Kayla and Janet had finally paired up ahead of them and he wasn't about to disturb them.

Grace opened her eyes and smiled. She didn't look any older than Kayla today—well, maybe a little, but only in the most attractive way. Grace could still pass for twenty, especially in the nice sweater and tailored pants she had bought for the occasion. He was sorely tempted to lean down and kiss her.

"I'm sorry, what was the question?" Grace asked. So maybe she wasn't all that solid after all.

"Just wondered what was going on in there," Carl said, tapping her softly waved blond hair.

Her brow creased in a tiny frown. "If you must know, I was praying."

Of all the answers Carl had expected, this wasn't one of them. "'Praying'?"

"Yes. You didn't know I did that, did you?" Grace actually stuck her tongue out at him. Seeing her do that shot an electrified thrill through Carl. This woman would be the death of him, or at least his common sense, yet.

"What were you praying about, Grace?"

"Everything, I guess. Asking God to be as good to Kayla and Bill, and Janet, as he's been to me. To smooth the way before them. It can't be very easy, you know, Carl."

"We all know that." Carl could feel himself shutting down emotionally. He knew that Grace's admission should have had the opposite effect on him. He should be jubilant that she was finding her way clear to walk with God. Instead, why did this make him feel jealous of the very God they both loved?

He was so shaky he could barely look at Grace. Until she squeezed both his hands and he looked directly at her instead of into the sunshine with its drifting dust motes. Her eyes held the same dancing golden flecks—and a promise that everything would be all right. Standing there, holding her warm hands, turning the thin gold band on her left ring finger, Carl felt his fears ease. He didn't know how long that comfort would hold up in the face of everyday life once they left this place, but for now he believed that the Lord would provide for them both. And for now, it was enough.

Chapter Fourteen

"**Y**ou gave away our rooms?" Carl stood staring at the motel clerk. "But I reserved them in advance. With my credit card."

It was ten o'clock at night. Too late to go anyplace else. Nobody was in any shape to drive the three hours home. He wouldn't trust Kayla or Janet with his truck, no matter what. Grace looked as tired as he felt. Now what did they do?

"Well, not all of them, exactly," the desk clerk admitted.

"So what, exactly, do we have?" Carl didn't shout. He was very calm, under the circumstances.

"Uh, one room. It *does* have two double beds." The clerk brightened.

"Great. We'll take it. The girls can share somehow, and I'll sleep in the truck." Carl put his credit card down on the counter, signed in and went to break the news to the ladies.

The ladies took it better than he'd expected. Even after he'd escorted them to the room and they'd looked at its small confines, nobody complained.

"Hey, it will be like a giant slumber party. No problem." Of course Kayla was used to giant slumber parties. "And it's too cold for you to sleep out in the truck, Mr. Brenner. I mean, can't we get a foldout bed or something?"

Grace called the front desk. "No rollaways. But I agree with Kayla, it's too cold to sleep out in the truck. Besides, you're the one paying for the room. You should at least get to sleep in it." She sounded braver than she looked.

Grace's voice was firm with conviction, but her eyes told Carl how much trepidation she had about sleeping in the same room with him, under any circumstances.

It was Janet who surprised them all. "This is ridiculous. We're four adults here, and we all need a good night's sleep. Kayla and I will take one bed, and you two can sort things out with the other one. I don't care if you share it, or sleep on the floor or whatever. I do know it's been a long day and I want to get out of these dress shoes and into my sweats and fuzzy socks. And honestly, I'm too tired to care about what everybody else does tonight.''

Carl looked at Bill's mother from a new vantage point. Maybe she wasn't the dried-up old prune he'd figured her for. Janet was actually being practical and sensible. And it had been a very long day.

After the involved graduation ceremony and a reception, Bill had shown them around the base. Bill had held Kayla's hand in his almost the entire afternoon and evening and he looked, well, like a man now in his military haircut and dress uniform. Maybe that is what Janet had seen too. That this was a time to move on with life and she better get going.

But regardless of the day's events, Carl was still in a strange situation. Sharing a motel room with three women was beyond his realm of experience. As far as that went, sharing a motel room with *one* woman was beyond his experience. What a way to start.

Now that the situation was settled to their satisfaction, the three women were bustling around the room, kicking off heels and working out a bathroom schedule so they could all take turns at bubble baths and makeup removal or whatever. Carl found himself just watching. It was Grace, of course, who caught his eye. She could apparently feel his gaze on her, because she stopped padding across the room's lush carpet and looked over her shoulder at him.

"I'll take the floor. Surely there are enough blankets to make some kind of bed with."

"Oh, come on, Grace. You know what that's going to do to your back." Kayla sounded more like her older sister than a teenager. "Besides, like Janet says, we're all adults. We know nothing's going to happen here except sleep. And I don't know about anybody else, but I'm sure ready for that."

Grace had a strange expression on her face. Carl thought it probably mirrored his own. She looked as if she wanted to argue with Kayla, but was too embarrassed somehow. In the end she shrugged and started rooting through her overnight case. "Fine. I expect we can share a double bed during a giant slumber party, huh, Carl?" She challenged him to say anything to the contrary.

"Sure. Right. We're all adults." Carl really hoped his voice didn't crack. "Hey, if we both take a blanket and a couple of pillows, we probably won't even know we're sharing the bed."

Right. Grace's silent look told him everything. She knew that at home he had a queen-size mattress all to himself. This was going to be a long night and an interesting one. How early did it get light at this time of year? Carl groaned inwardly, then went to his suitcase for the flannel pants and

T-shirt he'd packed to hang out in. It had been bad enough when he'd figured he was sharing an adjoining room with the three women all next door. This was going to be sheer torture.

She was going to die, or go crazy or something before she went to sleep.

Grace lay on her right side, facing out toward the cool air in the room, willing herself to go to sleep. But all she could do instead was concentrate on Carl's hand. Spread out over her entire side, it spanned her body protectively. And even through the layers of T-shirt and blanket that separated them, it was a very warm hand.

Just the warm, even pressure of his thumb under her shoulder blade, those fingers splayed out against her ribs, the smallest finger somewhere down by her hipbone, was going to drive her mad.

It was so quiet she could scarcely hear Kayla or Janet breathe. Why couldn't either of them snore for distraction? Instead, they'd both put on sweats and slipped under the covers quickly, leaving Grace her turn in the bathroom. She'd come out, switched off the remaining light, and announced she was going up to bed, feeling flighty and awkward.

Now she tried to distract herself with thoughts of anything but the room and its occupants. How were the animals doing at home? Had Larry remembered to come over and feed them, and let the dog out? She suspected that when they got home she'd find both animals curled up together in the kitchen for warmth.

Warmth wasn't something she herself needed more of right now. It was hard not to fling off the covers and suck in the cool night air. The man was a living blast furnace. Carl positively radiated warmth, had it coming out the tips of his fingers to trace patterns on her already-fevered skin.

How on earth did she expect to sleep in the same bed with this man and not make an absolute fool of herself? Maybe if she tried to match her breathing to his, steady and calm behind her, she could go to sleep instead of lying here, rigid and alert, with Carl's hand reminding her just what she was missing.

Was he totally without feelings? Grace was still willing herself not to gasp or scream with each small movement of the bed under them, or of the man beside her—and he was asleep. She just couldn't see how anybody could drop off that quickly and uneventfully in a roomful of people. She knew that she herself would still be awake at dawn, counting the stars as they paled, then listening for the cry of a rooster in the distance.

If nothing else, the warm, sweet breath on the back of her neck was going to drive her to distraction. She felt so safe in Carl's arms. Safe from the world, at least—not safe from Carl. Except that she was probably safe there, too, given the speed with which he'd fallen asleep.

Or at least she thought he was asleep. Surely nobody that still, with breathing so regular, could be awake. Or could Carl be doing just what she was doing—willing himself to go to sleep so that he didn't pounce on her as willingly as she wanted to roll into his pounce? She shifted ever so slightly against the even pressure of the hand on her rib cage. It closed in almost convulsively, drawing her closer to his warm body. Feeling oddly gratified by his response to her sharing his bed, Grace snuggled her protesting body even closer to his large, warm, welcoming frame. Carl groaned softly. His whisper was so low, only she could hear. "I'm gonna die from this, you know, Grace. The waiting will kill me."

"At least we'll both die happy, Carl," she told him. "Because if the waiting doesn't kill you, I may wear you to the bone once we stop waiting."

It was the growl low in his throat that warned Grace, but not quickly enough to escape the hand that covered her side. She wondered which of the children had told Carl she was ticklish. One of them had, and she would find the culprit when they got home tomorrow and wring his or her sweet neck. Because he knew unerringly which spot to tickle to make her a helpless mass next to him.

"We will wait. It may kill both of us, but we will wait, Grace," he whispered in her ear a moment later while he still had her in a tight embrace. "I don't want to give anybody in Redwing the satisfaction of thinking we had to get married for the sake of a child."

"I'll agree with you on that one. And I'll agree with you on the other part, too, Carl."

"Which part would that be?" he asked, insinuating himself even closer to her.

"The part that's going to die if we wait too long. Thank heavens this is only for one night. Another night or two of this would kill me." How she ever fell asleep that way, with the dratted man behind her chuckling softly every once in a while, Grace couldn't imagine. She only knew that once morning came and she woke up, they were still joined together in a warm embrace. And both of them seemed to wake up smiling.

"Can I come out yet?" Carl sounded like a little kid kept out of a party. He sent all of them into fits of giggles, Grace the most.

"Not yet." Kayla sat down on her bed. "I'm still putting on my socks."

"And I'm still fastening—"

"Too much information, Janet." His strained voice through the bathroom door made them all giggle again.

"Just hold your horses." Grace looked in the mirror, checking to be sure everything was in place. It had made more sense for the three of them to change clothes together in the room while Carl hid out in the bathroom, but he was getting antsy in there. "You don't want to see us without our faces on, do you?"

"I've already seen you without your faces." Carl made a sound that might have been a snort. "Now, if you're down to a point where there are no other surprises there, I'm coming out."

"Then come on out." Kayla caught her hair up in a stretch band and made a ponytail. "There's nothing to see anyway."

The door opened. Carl came out looking like a rooster with his feathers ruffled. "I knew that before."

"Are you hungry?" Grace was trying so hard not to let her laughter escape while she changed the subject. She couldn't look at him. If she did, she wasn't going to be able to hold in this traitorous giggle. "I'm hungry. In fact I'm starved. I think I'll go down and see what there is for breakfast." She left the room quickly, leaning on the wall down the stairwell for support. She mustn't laugh. She mustn't.

When strong arms grabbed her from behind, she was so startled she shrieked instead. "It's all right. Laugh," Carl said, before burying her in a moist kiss. "I tell you, woman, I'm going to die of want-ing you." And there on the stairwell he proved with a kiss that took her breath away that he wasn't as near death as he'd claimed.

The day stretched on like a desert. There wasn't another moment that Grace was alone with Carl until they'd deposited Janet and Kayla at home, picked up the kids from the Petersons', fed every-one dinner and made over the animals. Even then, the evening was full of reading to Maria, running over Spence's spelling words, making sure every-body had the right clean clothes for school the next morning. They had lost their normal "family" weekend. *How had this happened so quickly?* It wasn't losing the weekend that mystified Grace. It was the speed with which she and Carl and the children had become a family to each other.

Finally Spence went up to bed and Grace sat with a cup of tea. Carl took the dog out for a short walk in the brisk night air. When he came back his hair was rumpled. He sat down heavily in the arm-chair facing Grace.

"I don't know about you, but I regret giving in to peer pressure this weekend." His face was com-pletely somber and serious.

Grace didn't know whether to believe him or not. "I should have slept on the floor."

"No, like Kayla said, that would have been bad

for your back. But Grace, I don't think those two had any idea what they were doing to us.''

"I didn't have any idea what I was doing to us until it was two in the morning." Suddenly it was more comfortable to look at the curtains or the white mug that held her tea—anywhere but Carl's flushed face.

"Yeah, well, me neither. At least we don't have to worry about compatibility." His voice held laughter. "So are you still serious about finding your Aunt Jo before we get married?"

"Yes, I am."

"Then we'd better do it quickly. Is there anything you haven't told me that might be of help finding her? So far, the easy stuff hasn't worked."

"Well, she moved around a lot when she was a girl. She always said her dad never liked being near his neighbors. So they went different places. When she married Mr. Sparks, she settled down for a while. Said it felt strange." Grace could see Jo, sitting in the rocker that now nestled in the corner of Carl's bedroom, telling her stories.

"Where was she the happiest, do you think?"

"Maybe near a place called Kingdom City. She always said the house they had there was the prettiest thing she ever saw." Casting her mind back to Jo and her stories, Grace could almost hear her aunt's homey laughter.

"Yes, probably Kingdom City or around there.

I don't know why that was the best place for her, because my uncle was a trucker, always in and out, and they never had two nickels to rub together. Maybe it was because that's where he's buried. When Mama came back with me, or just about to have me, they moved again because it was a tiny little place. At the time Aunt Jo had her mother-in-law with her. She figured with three women and a new baby, they needed someplace bigger. Then, after they moved, the old Mrs. Sparks died and Mama didn't stay long, so there was Aunt Jo, with me alone in this big old place out in the country. Oh, if I had a nickel for every time she said she wished she'd never moved…''

The tears came then, but not for the reasons Carl probably suspected. Jo had always wished they'd stayed put so that Matt Mallory wouldn't have wandered into their lives. She had never liked him and his stealing of her girl. And it hadn't taken long for Grace to agree with her, even though she and Jo had never admitted that to each other.

Carl leaned between their chairs and gently wiped her tears away. ''I was afraid of this. I'm really sorry I can't find any more. But nothing in that whole mess had a return address on it except the last letter you had. And when I found a post-master there, he was somebody who had taken over after your aunt moved, and he didn't know.''

Carl caressed her face. It felt so good to lean her

cheek into his warm, callused palm. "Can you think of the name of the place?"

Grace shook her head, dismayed that it all came down to this. "There wasn't one, exactly. It was just a little settlement of a few houses and not much else in Southern Missouri. Not a town, really. There were towns you could walk to, seven or eight miles away. Valle Mines, I think. And there was another one."

Carl's hand moved convulsively beneath her cheek. His skin was pale when she looked at him, and his eyes had a faraway unfocused look. "Big Springs, maybe?"

"That sounds right."

"Then that's where we'll try first. But don't get your hopes too far up."

"I won't. I really appreciate what you've done already. It's a wonderful gift," she told him.

He moved his hand and shook his head briefly, the way Four did when he lost the track on a rabbit. "Well, it's good so far. But I can't make any more promises. Big Springs, of all places." With that, he went to the computer, where he buried himself for the evening. Grace finished her cold tea while she watched him. She wanted to ask what was so unusual about Big Springs, but she didn't. When Carl was ready to tell her, he would. Wouldn't he?

Chapter Fifteen

Four days. That was all it took him to find her. Carl stared at the screen in front of him, unable to move or speak. How could this be? When he'd done searches for himself, nothing this good had *ever* come up. It just wasn't fair.

The blinking arrow of the cursor on his screen mocked him. Four days. And not even whole days at that—just time snatched here and there between jobs at the store. He was almost too busy selling new summer clothes for every kid in town to do this at all. And yet he'd found Jo Sparks.

There was a bitter taste in his mouth, like coffee that had been on the burner way too long. After twenty years of trying, he still couldn't find Danny. But he could find Grace's aunt in less than a week. Carl moved the cursor over to the Print Screen button. The printer hummed for a moment, then a sheet with the name and address and phone number he'd found curled out of the machine. He made a second copy. This way if he gave in to the temptation to burn the first one and not tell Grace anything, he would still be okay.

What was he thinking? Nothing was okay. This was the beginning of the end of his calm, peaceful life with a family. *It had been good while it lasted.*

Carl grabbed the papers from the printer tray. Time to get this over with, quick, before he lost his nerve.

He appeared in the kitchen like a ghost, silent and grim. The coffee mug she was washing slipped out of Grace's fingers and hit the sink mat with a thump. "Bad news?" Her mouth was so dry she could barely get out the words.

His gray eyes were flat, expressionless. "Not exactly. But what would you say if I asked you to marry me now?"

He had found Jo, but she was dead. It was all Grace could think. "I'd say it was still too soon. And I'd say I still want you to find Jo first. Unless you already have, and she's...dead."

Tears hotter than the dishwater under her fingers sprang up to burn Grace's eyes. That was it, she was sure of it. Jo was dead and Carl wanted to marry her to take her mind off it.

"No, Grace, she's not dead. At least I don't think so. If she is, she died after she paid last month's phone bill and electric service."

Grace wanted to leap, to dance. "So you did find her? Then why didn't you just tell me?"

Carl shrugged. "Because I know what's going to happen now."

Grace wiped her hands on the towel next to the sink. "Oh, do you? What's going to happen now, Carl?"

"Now you leave. I've found your aunt, and she's your family. Not like me. Let's face it, Grace, you may be wearing my ring, but basically we're still strangers. And blood is thicker than water."

Her hands were still damp. Grace ran them down the sides of her jeans, trying not to show all the aggravation she felt. "You don't think much of me, do you?"

He couldn't meet her gaze. "It's what *I* would do."

"Well, it's not what I would do. Not now, not later."

"Maybe. There's a lot you don't know about me."

Anger flared in Grace. "If there's so much I don't know about you, why should I marry you to begin with? When were you going to tell me all these secrets, anyway, after we got married?"

"That wouldn't be fair. But I'm afraid, Grace."

In Carl's expression, she could see the lonely boy again that had haunted her at Christmastime.

Grace sighed. "Afraid of what?"

"That once you really know me, all about me, you won't want to stay—no matter what. That marrying me would be out of the question."

Grace turned back to the sink. "For once, let me be the judge of that. Maybe I'm a more forgiving person than you think I am. Even if I'm not, maybe this God you've led me back to will give me the strength to be one.

"I'm making a pot of coffee. Then we're going to sit in the living room until I know everything there is to tell about you, even if it takes all night."

Carl enveloped her in a wordless hug, wrapping his arms around her spine. She leaned her head back, resting against his shoulder.

He was warm and so gentle. Grace couldn't imagine anything he could tell her that would drive her away. But then, Matt Mallory had looked like a nice young man at first. Maybe she was just a lousy judge of character— *No!* Living those years with Matt had made her an excellent judge of character. Carl might not be perfect, but who was? Grace filled the coffee carafe with water. Better make a full pot. This promised to be a rough talk.

Grace finished half a cup of coffee before the silence got to her. "Okay, let's start with the basics. Ever been in prison?''

"No."

"Killed anybody? Been divorced? Have illegitimate children in four counties?''

"Lord, Grace, *no* to all of the above.''

She put down her coffee mug and moved herself face-to-face with Carl on the couch. Grace took both his hands, marveling again at the way they enveloped hers. ''What is so awful that you can't tell me, then?''

He couldn't meet her gaze. Grace felt fingers of panic grip her insides. What sins had she missed in her litany?

"You know how I told you my family died in a fire?''

"When you were five," Grace prompted. "I remember.''

"Well, they didn't all die in the fire.''

She felt lost. ''Okay, explain that. Do you mean that you still have family someplace, or that the family you lost didn't really die in a fire?''

Carl sighed. ''Both, I guess. But how they died is the important part. As far as wanting to marry me is concerned, for sure. Danny's just a reason for not marrying you at all.''

Grace felt a pain in the middle of her forehead. She was wrinkling her brow together so hard that it hurt in an effort to concentrate on making sense of what Carl was saying. "Let's start at the beginning, Carl. Who's Danny? And how did your parents die?"

He ignored her first question. "We lived out in the country. Big Springs was the closest town. My father shot my mother." His voice was wooden, mechanical. "Then he set fire to the house, and shot himself. He didn't expect us to get out, I don't think."

Grace felt as if she had a clue now. "Us being..."

"Me and my brother, Danny. I was five, he was two. I lost him, Grace. I was supposed to take care of him, but I lost him."

Carl's tears devastated her. She was too small to take him totally in her arms and make his pain go away. Grace did what she could, wrapping herself around him for comfort. What should she do now?

Wait. Watch. Pray. And love. Holding Carl in her arms, Grace felt hot tears course down her face. She'd cried more since meeting Carl than she had in her whole life. But they were mostly healing tears.

Something inside her was letting go as she wept. With each step she took toward Carl, she felt closer to God, as well. And as she accepted God back into her life more and more, it was easier to put her burdens on Him. Carl's problems didn't sound earth-shattering when she had Jesus to lean on.

She held on to Carl, stroking his hair. Aunt Jo had always said there were no coincidences in God's world. *Maybe everything that had happened was for a reason.* Was this what it was for? All the suffering she'd gone through? Was there really a purpose to all that pain, after all? If this was the reason for that pain, it was worth it.

"Nothing you've said so far makes me love you any less, Carl." Her words were soft and shaky, but Grace managed to choke them out.

Carl's eyes sparkled with unshed tears. "How can you say that? I just told you my father was a murderer. That's the kind of background I come from. And the one thing I could have done to make things right—*the one thing*—I failed at. I couldn't even keep track of my own brother. Grace, he's twenty-eight years old, and I haven't seen him in twenty-six years!"

Grace felt understanding dawning in her. "Is that why you didn't want to tell me about Jo? You were jealous about Danny?"

"She was so easy to find. Everybody for someone else is always so easy to find." There was a note of childlike pain in his voice. "Why can't I find Danny? Why can't I have a family?"

"Like everybody else. Like me." Grace smoothed his hair and pulled him closer, as she would Spence. "Ah, Carl, you need to keep talking. This time, start at the beginning and tell me the whole story.''

But where did the whole story start? Carl stayed in Grace's arms, struggling to collect his thoughts. ''We have some things in common. My dad was in Vietnam, too. I don't remember him being around much when I was small. My mom raised me, and it was peaceful that way. He must have come back at least once, because there was Danny.''

This was hard. Carl pulled back to his own end of the couch. He couldn't move far enough to escape the old pain. ''Dad didn't come back the same guy who left.''

''A lot didn't.''

''Yeah, well, he was one of them. Even at age four I knew things weren't right. Mom tried to protect us from him as much as possible.'' He could still remember hiding in a darkened room. Danny was in the crib; he was scrunched under it. The noises outside the room were ugly.

''What happened?'' Grace reached over and grabbed his hand again. Carl took it like a lifeline.

''He wasn't in his right mind anymore. And he drank, I know. One night they got into it. The next thing I knew, I heard a bang. I knew somehow that we had to get out of there. The neighbors found us out in the snow, watching the trailer burn.''

"What happened to Danny?"

"We went to the same foster home at first in Big Springs. But I was bad, disruptive. The people didn't want to keep me. They split us up. Then I kept running away, trying to find the first place we'd stayed together."

Grace sat up sharply. "How old were you?"

"Six."

"And they didn't give you counseling?"

"Nope. For a while they put me in some kind of juvenile home, but that was about the extent of any treatment I got." Carl let go of her hand.

"One day when I was older than Spence, I had a visitor. It was my Uncle Jim, my mother's brother. He apologized for not getting there sooner, not knowing what we'd gone through."

"Where had he been?"

"Overseas. Stationed in Germany with the army. He hadn't been allowed to come back for the funeral, and had gotten the impression somehow that my dad had killed us all. When he came back to the States and found out that wasn't true, he came to find me."

"Wow. Did he take you away from the foster home then?"

"Not that day. There was legal stuff he had to work through. As soon as he could, though, he did. We came here to Redwing, where he'd bought the store."

"But he didn't find Danny?"

"Not a trace. It's like the kid vanished, Grace. I've looked every way I know how to. Once I left that first foster home, it's as if he fell off the face of the earth."

Grace pulled him into her arms again. Carl didn't resist. "Does this mean you gave up?"

"Not really. I still try once in a while. Every time I find somebody for someone else, it makes me look again. But I'll never find him, Grace."

Her eyes blazed. "How do you know? How can you say that?"

"Because God doesn't want me to. I mean, I've asked Him, more times than I care to count. Let me find him. Let me have a family. And here I am." It tore him up to admit that much to her, but it was the truth.

"I don't believe that."

"What? That God doesn't answer every prayer? That sometimes we just ask too much and he says no?"

Grace pounded a fist into her open palm in frustration. "That is not the God you've shown me, Carl. It's definitely not the God that my aunt always talked about."

"So explain what wonderful reason God has for keeping me apart from the only family I have."

Grace's expression was blank. "I don't have any idea. Maybe so you could give me a family again.

You know that's what you've done. Given me a family."

Her face became more animated. "When you came to my house, things could have gone a whole different way. You should have been coming to take Matt—I mean Spence—to one of those juvenile halls you remember."

"I couldn't do that, just because I remember them too well."

"So instead we have a home now, and a stable situation. And you found Jo for me, when I didn't know how." She took his hands again. Her face was as earnest as a child's. "If you give me the chance, I will be your family. I know that won't replace the one you've lost. But I want to be with you through whatever happens next."

He pulled her into a tight embrace. The woman had such tiny bones, it felt like holding a bird. Yet, like a bird's, those bones had the strength of steel. Grace was strong enough to stand up to this crisis and any other. "Maybe you're right about God, after all." Carl knew his words were muffled, spoken into her soft hair as he crushed her to him.

He had knocked over one of their coffee cups. The liquid was running across the hardwood floor. Carl moved quickly, grabbing a throw rug to soak up the mess. As he did, the flash of white paper caught his eye.

"I never did give you this, did I?" He held out

the crumpled sheet to Grace. "That's the address I found, and the phone number."

Grace took it with shaking hands. "How could anyone but God make things like this possible, Carl? And how could He not make all things possible in time? We'll find Danny. Maybe we were just supposed to do it together."

Carl felt small in the face of her optimism. He wished he could share it. "Go call her. I'll finish with the floor."

Grace seemed to be in a daze. She held the paper as if it were gold-plated. "I think I will. Now." She got up and walked out of the room. Carl stayed and wadded up the sodden throw rug. The mug he picked up struck the arm of the couch. Heavy china, it didn't chip, just rang with a hollow sound. *Just the way you feel.*

Chapter Sixteen

Her hands were still shaking. Grace put the phone down, took a deep breath. It was all she could do to pick it up again, punch in the numbers.

It startled her when the phone rang on the other end. Surely any moment now she'd hear that grating tone instead, and the too-smooth voice of the operator, telling her she's dialed a no-longer-in-service number.

Three rings. Four. A pause and then a sound so incredibly sweet, Grace was nearly in tears again. "This is Jo, except it's this danged machine instead. You probably know how it works better than I do, so leave your name and number. Unless you want to sell me something. Then just hang up."

Jo was still her old feisty self. Grace waited for the end of the series of clicks and beeps that meant she should leave her message. "Aunt Jo? It's me, Grace." She probably didn't have much more time. She repeated Carl's phone number into the machine. "Call me. Hurry." Her hands were still trembling when she hung up the phone.

Grace stayed there and slept in the kitchen chair, slumped over the table. When she woke in the morning, stiff and sore, she resolved to get Carl a cordless phone. That way she could take the handset to bed with her if the call didn't come this morning.

Who was she kidding? If the call didn't come before noon, she'd need more than just a cordless phone to hold on to her sanity. Grace looked out the window at the pale spring dawn. "Keep her in Your care, God, wherever she is. And please, let her call back soon." It was all she could do. Only God could do the rest.

"What's wrong with Mom?" Only Carl was supposed to hear Spence's comment at the breakfast table, Grace was sure. When she turned around from the stove and looked at her son, he ducked his head.

"Mom is waiting on a phone call. And she's nervous. Carl found Aunt Jo, but she wasn't home last night when I called. And she hasn't called me back."

"And it's driving you nuts, huh, Mom?" Spencer's expression was serious. "Are we really going to get to see her again?"

"That's what I want. If I knew she was home, I'd get out my maps and be on the road."

Carl shook his head. "In that car? I wouldn't trust that thing to the county line. When you go, Grace, take the truck. Or I'll go with you and we'll all take the truck."

"You just want to make sure I come back." Grace wished she could have taken back the words the moment she spoke. Carl looked as if she had slapped him.

"I'm sorry. I shouldn't have said that." She turned off the burner on the stove and hurried to his place at the table.

Both kids were goggle-eyed. Grace could see their silent question to each other. What was going to happen now? But unlike what they'd witnessed before with Matt, with Carl she could use humor to ease the tension.

She leaned down and kissed Carl on the forehead. It put her face nearly upside down in front of his to kiss him there. While she was at a disadvantage he reached up and grabbed her in a cockeyed bear hug of his own.

"You're right. Halfway, at least. I don't *just* want you back, but it is a good observation on your part. I would also worry about you less if you took the truck. It won't break down in the hundred miles or so between here and Big Springs, unlike that car. I'd still rather you made sure Jo was home first.''

This was it? This was how mature, rational folks resolved their differences? Grace felt elation. Or was it just the effect of being upside down? "Okay, let go of me. All the blood is rushing to my head." Grace moved her head so that her hair, which now curtained both their faces, had to tickle Carl. "Come on, I mean it. I promise I won't take off in that old car. And I'll make sure Jo is home first.''

Maria was giggling. Spence obviously didn't know what to do. Adults who horsed around in the kitchen in a friendly manner were new to him. "Mom, your face is really red.''

"Yeah, well, have this lummox hold you upside down for a while and see what color your face is.'' Grace tried to sound grumpy.

"Cool. Can I?'' Carl lunged for Spence, who zipped around the table, laughing to avoid his grasp.

"Anybody who knocks over milk or syrup is scrubbing this kitchen. With no help from me, I might add.'' That didn't stop the chase around the table, but it slowed it down. Only after things calmed down and the kids were out the door did Grace realize what Carl had done. When Carl came back to the kitchen, ready to go to the store, she had to compliment him.

"Good job."

He stopped in the middle of the room, still in the act of tying the hated tie on his way out the door. "What do you mean?"

"We scared the kids there for a minute. Nice way to defuse things."

Carl shrugged. "You didn't get to have much of an opinion, uh, before, did you?"

"Not exactly. I was always too busy to have one if Matt wasn't there, and leery of voicing it if he was. It's taken some getting used to, being opinionated again."

"I think you're picking it up okay. Want to call Big Springs again?"

Grace looked away from him. His generosity continued to amaze her. "Yes. No. I don't know, Carl. What if she's just not picking up the phone? If she's just…given up on me after this long."

"I don't think so. From what little you've told me about your aunt, she wouldn't ever give up on you. I can call if you like."

"No, I'll do it." Grace used the kitchen phone, but she reached the machine again. Grace held on and left another message.

"I don't suppose there's any way I could talk you into coming to the store? I hate to think about you pacing the house all day, waiting for that phone to ring.''

"Not unless the telephone company around here has been modernized while I wasn't looking, and you can get this thing to do call forwarding.'' Grace glared at the silent instrument on the wall.

"If I could get them to do it just for you, Grace, you know I would.''

Grace looked into his silvery eyes. "You would, wouldn't you? You're a good man that way, Carl. Good in most ways. So go to work. If she hasn't called by the time school lets out, I'll come over and scream.''

"And if she does call, I'll probably be able to hear you scream from the store.''

The urge to stick her tongue out at Carl was overpowering. He brought out the child in her, in good ways and bad. But Grace had to admit he was right. If Jo called, everybody in about a mile radius would know once Grace got off the phone. It thrilled her that in this short a time, Carl knew that about her, and so much more.

"Mr. Brenner? I don't think this is right." Kayla held out a handful of bills. "I think you just gave me back in change what I should have paid for that shirt.''

Carl looked at the cash register, then at the

change in her hand. "You're right. Thanks for catching me on it."

"No problem. It's kind of cool. I never thought I'd have better math skills than you."

"Yeah, well, enjoy it, because it probably won't ever happen again."

Kayla smiled. "I bet you're right. I hope it gets better, whatever it is."

Carl's brow furrowed. "What do you mean?"

"Well, something has to have you awful spaced out to miss a simple sale like that. I figure you're either sick, or you and Grace had a fight or something."

"More like 'or something.'" Carl had no idea how to explain Jo Sparks and her phone call, or lack of it, to Kayla, who shrugged now as she headed out.

For that matter it was hard to explain to himself. He should be thrilled that Jo wasn't calling back. The longer this wore on, the longer he had Grace. No matter what she said, it was hard to believe that Grace would really choose Carl over her own family.

If somebody walked in here, today, and offered to trade him the whole store for finding Danny, Carl knew he'd give the store away. *What about Grace?* That was a tougher choice. If the only way to find Danny was to give up Grace and the kids, and what they had going for them, would he do it?

Maybe. Fortunately, nobody was asking him to make that choice. Nobody ever would, because he was never going to find Danny. He was, however, going to have to get used to the idea of giving up Grace and the kids. Because sooner or later Jo would call, or Grace would call and find her at home. Then this illusion of a family would be gone for good.

The bell over the door jingled. Spence and Maria were done with school. "Did Mom hear anything?" Spence had been running; it showed in his cheeks.

"Good afternoon to you, too. I'm fine. No cookies or anything from Miss Naomi, but it's been a pretty good afternoon—"

"Okay, already. Hi, Carl. How was your day? Mine was okay. I got an A-minus on my math test. Jennifer Brown got higher." Spence fairly wiggled with impatience. "Now, did Mom hear anything?"

"No, not yet." Before Carl could run Maria through the same drill, the phone rang. "Redwing Mercantile," he answered.

"I'm looking for Grace Mallory." The voice was soft, tentative. Just listening to it, Carl could picture an older woman. "Do I have the right number?"

"Yes and no," Carl said. "This is the store, and she's at the house. Can I give you that number?" He could hear a strange buzzing in the back of his head. Why didn't he just hang up, pretend this was a wrong number—anything?

"I think I already have it." The woman on the other end of the phone read back a number. "That's what I heard on the machine, anyway."

"Well, ma'am, I don't know if the machine is a little off or what, but you're not quite right on that number." Carl told her the right one, just one digit off from where she was to begin with. "Would this be Mrs. Sparks?"

"It is. Is there something the matter with my girl?"

"Not yet. But I may have to catch her when she picks up that phone at the house and hears your voice."

"Well, I hope it isn't far from the store to the house, because you're going to have some fast catching to do. And thank you, Mr., uh, I don't expect it's Redwing, is it?" There was laughter in her voice. Carl liked this woman in spite of himself.

"Nope. Not Mercantile, either." The cheerful voice on the other end of the line made Carl giddy instead of depressed. Grace would be so happy. "It's Brenner, Carl Brenner. And there's somebody here who wants to say hello before we hang up."

Spencer all but snatched the phone out of his hand. "Aunt Jo? That really you? Hey. No, not anymore. Mostly everybody calls me Spence. Right, I'm ten.'' He paused to listen, and Carl could guess what Jo was asking him. Something about Matt Mallory, from the way the kid's expression darkened. ''I better let Mom tell you about that. Love you, too. Yeah, I better race Carl home. Bye.''

''Are we going to?'' Spence asked after he hung up. ''Race home? Mom's gonna be a mess once she talks to Aunt Jo. I bet when we get there she's sitting in the middle of the kitchen floor. Probably bawling.''

''No bet on that one, bud. Flip over the sign on the front door to Closed for me. Maria, don't take off that coat, sweetheart. Where's your book bag?''

''Here. On the floor. Will we really have to catch her?'' Maria asked, looking somber.

''What, your mom? No, I don't think so. But I do want to be there pretty quick.'' Carl hoisted her up into his arms, and boosted her onto his back. ''Piggyback okay with you? I don't want to leave you behind.''

Spence was already out the door, the bell jingling madly in his rush. ''Cool.'' Maria giggled from her perch atop Carl. ''Let's go. Spencer's going to win.''

No, Grace was going to win. And suddenly Carl was glad for her, even if it meant letting go. He wanted nothing but the best for her, and if this was it, so be it. Maria was a sweet weight on his back. "Duck through the doorway. I don't want to take off any important body parts, like your head."

Her laugh was wonderful. Carl prayed it wasn't the last time he heard it. *Let me keep them, God.* It was his prayer all the way home, with the child bouncing in rhythm to his strides.

"See, I told you I wouldn't take a bet on that one." Carl put Maria down just inside the kitchen door. Spence already stood there, watching his mother. She sat on the floor. She was, as the kid had inelegantly put it, bawling. Wiping her wet face with one hand, she held the phone with the other.

Carl could only do one thing. He sat down on the floor with her, his back up against the kitchen cabinets. There was even a handle poking his spine in one place. Splaying out his legs, and wrapping his arms around Grace, he brought her body in close to his. Sitting there, without saying a word, he gave her the comfort he knew she needed as she talked to Jo.

Her body trembled. Carl leaned his forehead against her soft hair. He wanted her to know, in the most basic of ways, that he was there for her.

Apparently he wasn't the only one. Four sat in front of her. He kept offering Grace a large front paw, plopping it down on her knees. Without looking at him, Grace eased him off every time. She was concentrating on one thing only: the woman on the other end of that phone line.

"What? Of course we'll come. I have to talk to Carl first. He owns a store here, and he doesn't have any help at the moment but me. Yes, it would be hard to keep things open with both of us gone. We might be able to train Four to run the register, but he'll want to come meet you, too." Her laughter warmed Carl. "No, he's not a weird kid. He's a dog. A big yellow one. You'll love him."

The conversation went on. Carl tried to think about how to keep the store open if he took Grace to see Jo for a couple of days. Nuts. If he left Kayla in charge that long, the vultures would clean him out to the bare walls.

Maybe if they went on a weekend they'd be okay. At least he wasn't open on Sunday, so that would only give her Friday afternoon and Saturday to mess up the bookkeeping. Carl sat up straighter. Janet could help out on Saturday, too. She wasn't well trained in retailing, but she did have a lot more common sense than Kayla did. The two of them together might do okay. And hadn't Janet said she owed him one for the trip to Fort Leonard Wood? He'd better collect on the favor quickly while she still felt that way.

Grace was making her goodbyes now. Carl

heard her click off the phone, and she leaned into him.

"We're going. We're actually going."

"Soon, I hope. Because you'll be a basket case until we do."

"You're right. If there wasn't life to take care of, I felt like telling Jo we'd be there tonight. It's only a couple of hours away."

Something inside Carl tilted crazily. "So let's do it. If the kids miss a couple of days of school, so what? We can get Kayla to feed the cat, and I'll ask her and Janet to take over the store."

Grace's mouth hung open. She looked like a fish gasping for air. "Are you serious?"

"Yeah, I am. Better catch me quick while I still feel this way. You never know how soon I might decide this is a lousy idea after all."

Grace scrabbled around and hugged him, hard. "It's a wonderful idea. And you're a good man just for thinking it, Carl."

Just for that? Would she still consider you so decent if you didn't have these crazy ideas? Carl pushed away the questions. Nothing had been quite sane or normal since Grace Mallory had come into his life. Nothing at all lived up to his previous expectations anymore.

Sitting there, with Grace in his arms, he made a surprising discovery: he didn't want anything else.

That vague feeling of yearning wasn't constantly with him anymore.

He still missed Danny. And life running a store in Redwing, Missouri, wasn't all it could be. But with Grace in his arms those things didn't gnaw at him in the same way.

It was crazy, really. Having Grace here, so vibrantly here with her arms around him, making a bony, uncomfortable weight in his lap, was bliss. And he had just suggested that they get straight up off the kitchen floor and do the one thing that would take her out of his arms permanently—just because it made her happy.

He should have his head examined. Carl decided he'd do just that when he came home from Big Springs. He'd have plenty of time, anyway. Because he was still pretty sure he'd be coming back alone.

Chapter Seventeen

Grace's stomach fluttered. Why had she let Carl talk her into eating dinner? Even the one single hamburger she'd nibbled on sat in her stomach like a rock.

He and the kids hadn't had any problems eating. Neither had Four, blissfully chowing down a double burger with bacon and cheese in his crate in the back of the truck.

Nobody else was as nervous as she was. Of course, the dog never got nervous. Spencer was too excited about seeing Jo again to be upset about anything, and Maria sensed his excitement, not her mother's nerves.

Carl, driving the truck, had been very quiet. Was he still concerned that she would leave him to stay with Jo? Grace couldn't think of a way to bring the subject up. It was hard for her to imagine that he'd think that way.

Carl's signaling to turn off the highway pulled her out of her thoughts. "We're not there yet, are we?"

"Just to a rest stop. But we're close. Big Springs can't be more than five miles ahead, and Jo's directions put her place about two miles past that." Carl looked at her and Grace felt shock waves jolt through her from the reflection of feelings she saw in his eyes.

"So you want me to drive the last bit?"

Carl nodded. "If you could. For whatever reason, I don't feel up to it."

Grace knew it cost him to admit that. "No problem. Any detours you want me to make?"

Carl shook his head. "Not in the dark. Tomorrow in the light I will need to go exploring." He swung down out of the truck, leaving her to slide over the bench into the driver's seat.

He stretched as he followed the path around the truck, lit by headlights. Grace longed to hug him for comfort. But they were only seven miles from Jo! It was hard to imagine.

Carl got back into the truck. Impulsively Grace leaned over and kissed him, raising a flutter of giggles from the back seat. "Oh, stop, you two." She didn't even bother turning around to look at the kids.

"But it's so mushy up there."

Carl laughed. "You aren't going to believe me, but someday, my friend, you are going to want to be the guy in the front seat."

Spence didn't sound convinced. "No way."

Carl winked at Grace. It lifted her heart. "I know it will be a while, but someday that will happen. Not soon, I hope, but someday."

Spence made a sound like the cat coughing up a hairball. "I hope not soon, either. I mean, I'll kiss Aunt Jo when we get there, but kissing girls? No way."

"No girl would kiss you anyhow," Maria piped up.

That started Grace giggling in the front seat as she pulled back onto the highway. Seven miles and counting. It felt like seventy miles instead. She resisted the impulse to smash down on the gas pedal. If she got a speeding ticket right outside Big Springs, she'd never hear the end of it.

Spence sighed. "Why does Maria have to pick on me?"

"Because she's your kid sister. It's her job," Carl explained, and Grace could hear a thread of pain in his voice. "Heck, I'd give anything if I could have my kid brother back to rat on me."

It was all Grace could do to keep her eyes on the road. Carl was so natural with the kids, and took them into his confidence so readily.

"You have a brother? Cool."

"It would be cooler if I'd seen him growing up. I haven't seen him since I was younger than Maria."

"That's rough." Spence's voice held real compassion and Grace was proud of her son. "At least you had a brother for a while. Do you know what it's like to be the only guy in the house?"

"Yes, I do. And I'm glad I'm not anymore, and I'm glad you're not anymore. We've got to stick together, huh, Spencer?"

"For sure. I figure if you stick around long enough we can talk Mom into getting married. Then maybe we can get the majority around here."

Grace nearly swerved off the road listening to her son's logic. "Hey, I just thought of something," the boy added. If you count Four, we already have the majority."

Grace laughed. "Not for long. The score is about to be tied. About a mile up the road is Aunt Jo's house, and even counting the dog, we'll be tied again."

"That's okay. Aunt Jo's on my side anyway. I remember her spoiling me rotten when I was a little kid."

"And you can hardly wait for her to start doing it again." Grace felt a kinship with her son. As she got closer to Jo's door, she was a child again, too. And oh, how she was ready to be spoiled rotten.

* * *

Organized chaos? Controlled pandemonium? Carl wasn't sure how to describe the scene in front of him. He and the dog stood on Jo's gravel driveway just far enough from the melee not to get squashed.

Jo was a substantial lady. Her red hair, streaked with white, didn't seem to owe anything to store-bought coloring. Maria had already launched herself into Jo's arms—a sure sign that she must be okay. The child looked natural there, clinging to the woman who was as close to a grandmother as she was likely to get on this earth. After Jo planted a resounding kiss on her cheek, Maria shimmied down to the gravel again, jumping up and down beside her.

Grace and Jo couldn't stop chattering, hugging, separating and starting the whole process over again. Maria and Spence were right in the middle of it. Four wished he were, too. Carl could tell by the way he whined and pulled at the hand on his collar.

"I don't think so. Any more weight and that pile is likely to bowl right over." Carl tried to imagine adding an eighty-pound dog to the clump of people in front of him. It wasn't a pretty sight.

"Ah, he's feeling left out. Well, come on over." Jo bent down and patted her knees. Her studded-denim skirt pooled around her as she coaxed the dog. "C'mon. A little dog slobber never hurt anybody."

Four understood her tone, if not her words. He bounded over, his entire back end wagging. When he knocked Jo over onto her rear in the gravel, everyone laughed but Carl.

"Now don't you fuss at him." Both of Jo's hands, with their glossy red nails, twined in the dog's fur at ear level. The animal appeared to be laughing with the people. "I asked him over here."

"I know. But he knows better." Carl came closer and Four sat without being told. Jo let go of his feathery ears and extended a hand to Carl.

"If you want to apologize, just help me up off the pavement. Then we'll get you all inside instead of standing out here in the dark and the cold."

Carl helped her up. Jo's eyes glittered with happiness. "I didn't mean to get a hug from the dog before I got one from you."

"That's okay. He's friendlier with strangers." Carl winced at how his own words came out.

"You're no stranger. You brought me back my girl!" Jo's embrace was strong, and she smelled of one of the sweet perfumes on Doc's counter. "Now come inside before we all get chilled."

Carl couldn't imagine anybody being chilled around the warmth of Jo Sparks. But with her hand on his sleeve he wasn't going to argue. He let himself be led into her front room.

Lamps glowed golden, making a place of welcome trimmed with homemade afghans and friendly knickknacks. In the daylight the room might look worn around the edges, but tonight it looked like home. Carl could tell it looked that way to Grace. She sank down in an armchair upholstered in rose plush.

"You're home," Carl said. The words came out sounding more cheerful than he'd expected they would.

Grace leaned back in the chair. "I am. For the first time in six or seven years. But I think I could say that about anyplace this particular chair, and Aunt Jo, were. Think it would fit in your parlor?"

Carl felt an overwhelming wave of feelings. This wasn't a plan he'd considered. "Sure. Do we have to keep it pink?"

"Old Rose," Grace corrected, settling deeper into the chair. "And yes, we do."

"Oh, no, we don't," Jo chimed in. "I've been waiting for eight years to have that chair reupholstered, young lady. Now that you've seen that I kept it that way for you, it goes into the shop pronto. It's a disgrace as is."

Grace stood. "But you kept my favorite chair just the way I remembered it, just for me."

Jo nodded. "I knew you'd be back. I waited and

prayed on it, and keeping that chair just the way it was seemed to be the way to tell myself I believed you'd be back. But Grace, honey, that plush has to go.''

They fell into each other's arms again, tears and laughter mixing. ''Does this mean that there are twin beds with chenille spreads in the guest room?''

''It sure does. I drew the line at keeping the throw rugs. But your bed is still in the spare bedroom. *And* that couch over there makes into a daybed, with a trundle that pops out.''

''Let's put the kids in the guest room and Carl in your room, Grace said. ''Then we can take the couch and the pop-up and talk all night without disturbing anybody.''

''Don't I get any say in this?'' Carl asked. ''I don't want to put Jo out of her own bed.'' The identical expressions on the two women's faces told him all he needed to know.

''Well, Aunt Jo, show me to your bedroom and let me unpack my suitcase. No sense in keeping you ladies from your chat.''

''You can stay up and talk with us as long as you like,'' Grace said magnanimously. ''However, there are two people here that need to put on pajamas and brush teeth and head for those beds in the guest room.''

Her statement was met with groans and protests from both sides.

"I'll get the suitcases," Carl offered. "Maybe we can compromise here. You guys put on your pajamas first, and then come back out to visit. That okay?"

"Sure. If we can go to the creek sometime tomorrow when it gets light. Aunt Jo says there are tadpoles." Spencer grinned.

"Once it gets light. And only if they stay outside. I am not sharing anybody's house with a tadpole." Grace shivered slightly.

"Aw, you never let them have any fun. Besides, it's my house. Don't I get a say as to who, or what, comes in it?"

"Not tadpoles. Please, not tadpoles."

Jo grinned, a sight that made her look a whole bunch like Grace. "Just for you, we'll keep the tadpoles outside. The dog can come in, can't he?"

"He's real well trained. Carl can tell him to go sit down anyplace and he'll do it."

"As long as you don't tell him otherwise. I have this sneaking suspicion that when I'm not home he sits on the sofa and keeps Grace's feet warm."

"He is very warm. But I don't usually let him up on the furniture, because I know you don't like it."

Jo laughed. "Neither of us have changed much, have we? You are still a sucker for any animal that has feet and fur, and I'm still taking in every-body.''

"Including animals without feet and fur. Thanks for keeping the tadpoles outside." Grace stood up and clapped her hands. It got the dog's attention, if nothing else. "Now, let's get everybody going," Grace said. "Carl, let out the dog while you bring in the bags. Kids, go with Aunt Jo to the kitchen for cookies."

Yes, Grace was home already. And like at any other time, once she'd made herself at home there was no lounging around for anyone. Carl headed for the door, with Four on his heels. "You can help me bring in the suitcases. There're enough for you to carry, too."

He knew that would earn him some remark from Grace. What surprised him was the fringed cushion that zinged past his head, hitting the door with a plop. "Hasn't she told you about her softball career?" There was laughter in Jo's voice. "I've still got the trophy her team won in the county finals the year she was fourteen."

Carl hurried outside before anything else fol-lowed the pillow. Four looked at him with ques-tions in his dark eyes. Carl reached down and pat-ted the silky head. "Don't ask me what's going on. I'm only an observer." And tonight there would be plenty to observe.

* * *

Grace didn't know what it was about Jo that put Carl so at ease. Whatever it was, she thanked God that Carl felt it. He sat in Jo's front room, sock-footed and wearing the old sweats and T-shirt he put on when the kids got into their pajamas. Her favorite pink chair looked tiny with him sitting in it.

It looked shabby, too. Jo was right about re-covering it. That was okay, really. It was Jo's chair, even though Grace had always thought of it as her own personal throne. And no matter what color or print they put on the outside of the chair, it would still be that haven of love.

True to her word, Jo set up the daybed and the pop-up unit with help from the kids. They looked on this whole night as a giant slumber party. It would certainly be more fun than the last one Grace had attended. She felt herself blushing, thinking about that night in the motel. Well, maybe not more fun, but definitely more comfortable.

"Maria's wonderful," Jo said, bringing Grace back to the present. "I'm so glad I got to meet her while she's still young enough to say anything."

Grace wrinkled her nose. "That may work against me once in a while."

Jo laughed. "Probably. But think of how much fun I'll have."

Carl squirmed in his chair and leaned forward,

thrusting his long legs out into the room. "How can you do it?"

Grace could tell by the look on her face that Jo didn't understand his question, either. "Do what?"

"Just sit there and laugh and talk. You missed eight years of each other's lives. Those years are gone. They'll never be back. Aren't you angry?"

Jo shook her head. Grace loved watching her do that, seeing those auburn-and-white curls bounce. It made her want to reach over and pat Jo's hair, the way she did when she was a child. "No satisfaction in that for me. My satisfaction is here under this afghan." Jo reached out a worn hand to Grace's knee. "When Grace and Matt disappeared on me, I was mad. So angry for a while that I couldn't see straight. But I put them in God's care. I knew that way that they would be safe."

"Even if you never saw them again?"

Jo's voice, when she answered, was choked with tears. "Even if I never saw them again. And I had to deal with that part of it. But no matter where they were, I knew they were safe in the hands of the Lord. And someday I'd see them again."

"But that someday might not have been in this lifetime. How did you deal with that?" Carl asked.

Jo just looked at Carl for the longest time. "Who have you lost? Who are you so angry with? That question didn't just come out of the blue."

"No, ma'am, it didn't." In tortured bits, he told

his story. It brought tears to Grace's eyes again, hearing it for the second time.

After he'd finished, Jo sat silently again for a while. When she finally spoke, she was slow and deliberate. "What if you never find him?"

"I don't know. I've got to."

Jo looked as if she wanted to say something, then changed her mind. When her question came, Grace was pretty sure it wasn't what she'd first intended to say. "How old did you say Danny was? About Grace's age, right?"

"Right."

"What if you couldn't find him because he had no idea anyone was looking?"

Carl's brow furrowed. "How could that be? He was almost three when we lost track of each other. He's twenty-eight now. He's got to know he's adopted."

Jo shook her head. "Not necessarily. The whole time you were telling me about looking for your brother, something played through my mind. Now, I'm not saying the little boy I saw was your brother, Danny. But the same thing could have happened to him."

Carl's face was grim. "Tell me."

Jo looked down at her hands in her lap. "Grace always knew we weren't her parents. She was old enough when her mama died to remember her some. But soon after that, Eddie and I wanted to adopt her. We wanted to make sure she knew how much we wanted to keep her. And that was the best way to show her, we thought.''

''Sure.'' Grace could tell Carl couldn't imagine where this was going. *She* couldn't, either.

''I still remember sitting in the waiting room of a little law office in the next town over from where we lived. We'd scraped up the money to do all the paperwork, and folks told us this man was the best for the money. So I sat in there, waiting, with Grace on the floor playing with toys I'd brought.

''Eddie couldn't take off until we went to court. There weren't any other men waiting that day either. But there was another woman. She looked as old as I did. And she had a beautiful little boy with her.

''We had to wait awhile, so naturally, we talked. It turned out we were there for the same thing. But where we wanted to do this to show Grace how much we wanted her, this lady said her little Michael wasn't ever going to know he was adopted.''

''Could she do that?''

''I imagine so. With enough money in a small town, you can do just about anything. The lady looked like money was no problem. And she loved the child. It showed in everything—the way she touched him, how he was dressed and the tone of her voice. But that boy probably doesn't know to this day that he's adopted.''

Jo stopped then and looked first at Grace, then at Carl. "Could you live with that, if the same thing had happened to Danny? Could you let go of him, knowing he was safe, well and loved, but would never know you existed?"

Carl exhaled a long, low sigh. "I don't know. I honestly don't know."

Jo stood and walked over to his chair. "It must be heavy."

"What?"

"Bearing that burden all by yourself."

Without a word, without a sound, tears made tracks down Carl's face. Jo knelt down beside him. Grace stayed still, seeing something between them that needed to happen without her. "When it gets light, let's all go out together. I want to see where you lived near here. And maybe there, we can find a way to lay that burden down."

"Okay. It isn't that much longer, is it? Until it gets light."

"Only a couple of hours," Jo said. "We've been up most of the night." Grace was shocked when she looked at the clock on the mantel. Had they all really talked that long?

"Weeping may last the night," Jo said softly. "But joy comes in the morning. Morning's coming, kids. Let's get some rest before it gets here."

Chapter Eighteen

Grace figured they'd have to drive around for a while. She couldn't imagine having been away from someplace as long as Carl had been gone from Big Springs and being able to find what he was looking for right off the bat. Jo seemed to think otherwise. "You know where you're going?"

"Without using a map, once I get this close. I've come back in between times. Gotten as far as the highway, but couldn't bring myself to go down the road past that."

Grace reached out and squeezed his leg above the knee. "We'll all go together."

"We sure will. And we'll stay on the road if you don't hold on to my knee." The kids giggled in the back of the truck.

"Last time I try to reassure you."

"If you want to reassure me, hold on to my arm. But for now don't hold on to anything, because I think I see the turn coming up."

Woods and an occasional small house fronted the two-lane asphalt road. A couple of miles from the highway a narrow entrance led into a grid of small streets flanked by mobile homes. "People still live here," Grace said in surprise. She'd expected to find a burned-out shell, if anything, surrounded by woods.

"Yeah, about six generations of people removed from the folks that were here when we were. I know, because that was the first thing I checked when I was a teenager trying to find out what happened to my family."

"Your uncle wasn't any help?" Jo asked.

Carl shook his head. "He said everything was over and done. He didn't want my dad's name mentioned around him. I guess he thought I'd be better-off if I forgot."

"You weren't, though. Better-off, or even able to forget."

"Not for a moment," Carl said, sounding incredibly tired. They'd passed through the small area of streets and courts that made up the mobile-home park. On the far edge of the development, away from the main road, there was a spot where no one lived anymore.

Here was the emptiness Grace had expected to see. Carl stopped the truck in what would have been the original parking space. Past it, there was only worn, blackened concrete, pitted with age. Woods and scrub surrounded a small clearing behind the concrete pad.

"This is it." Carl opened the door, slid out of the truck. On the other side of her, Jo did the same. Grace opened the front-facing door to the back of the cab so that the kids and dog could climb out, too.

"Now don't get into any poison ivy," she warned. "And don't get anywhere near other dogs."

"We won't." Spence snapped the leash securely on Four.

"Stay out of any creeks back there. And stay within shouting distance," Carl said.

"Your shouting distance or Mom's?" Spence asked.

"Mom's." Carl's answer was quick and firm.

"Nuts. Okay. C'mon, Maria, before they think of any more rules." Spence and the dog headed off into the sparse woods, with Maria following.

Carl stood on the concrete. Grace tried to see whatever it was he saw with that glazed look. It had to be so horrible. When she was five she had a loving family, a home; everything was fine. What was it like to have had none of that?

"Do you want us to leave you for a few minutes?"

"Don't go far. But yes, I want to be alone for a little bit."

"We'll leave. But you won't be alone." Jo came up and put a hand on his shoulder. "Call if you need us. We'll stay in shouting range, like the kids."

She took Grace by the arm, and they walked down the asphalt road. It was half a city block before there were any home sites. "I wonder if people thought it was haunted," Jo said softly. "Folks are funny that way, after a tragedy."

"Not everybody. You never were," Grace replied. "You always pitched in when anybody needed something."

"I know. But most people just can't do that. I figured I didn't have much, but God gave me whatever I had for a reason, and it wasn't to sit on it like a chicken hatching eggs."

They walked down the lane a little farther. "You love him, don't you?" A breeze teased Jo's curls as she turned to look at Grace.

"I do. But I don't know what to do for him right now."

"Looks like you're doing all right. He didn't want to bring you here at first, did he?"

Jo always cut to the heart of the matter. "No," Grace admitted. "He's afraid I'll stay here with you. I told him that once I found you again, I'd marry him.''

''Good. You need each other.''

Grace wrinkled her nose. ''*I* need *him*. But I'm not sure Carl needs anybody. It seems so much like he's done all of the giving and none of the taking in our relationship. What do I do, Aunt Jo?''

''Just what you're doing. We walk a little farther, then we turn around. You try and give all this into the Lord's keeping, just like I asked Carl to do. Let Him sort it all out, Gracie. He's better at it than the rest of us.''

''I hope so. Because I feel really bad at it. Let's turn around and go back.''

Carl was leaning against the truck. His eyes were rimmed with red when Grace got close to him. She walked into his arms, and he wrapped them around her silently. He felt different somehow, as if there were barriers missing.

''Can you make your peace with this?'' Jo asked him.

''Not alone. But with God's help, and a good woman, I think I can.''

''Well, it looks like you've got both. And there's nothing that says you won't find that brother of yours yet. I imagine you'll still keep looking.''

Grace felt Carl's voice rumbling in his chest. ''You know I will.''

Jo tilted her head back at them. It seemed like another serious question was coming. "Is Redwing a decent place to live?"

Carl shrugged. Still buried in his embrace, Grace could feel his shoulders move up and down. He was not about to let her go. "It's okay. Why?"

"Because I gave this girl up once, and I'm not going to do it again. If I come for a wedding, I'm staying. There anyplace in town for an old lady to rent?"

Carl almost let go of her. "Probably. But if you come to Redwing you'll live with us. I'll remodel the rooms where Grace and the kids have been living so you can have your own place if you want."

"We'll talk about that later. Right now I'm going to go look for those kids and that dog. I know there's a little branch of a creek in these woods not too far back, and I can't imagine all three of them staying out of it."

Grace blessed her aunt for knowing what to say, and for knowing when to go. She looked up, still in the circle of Carl's arms. "You meant what you said?"

"Which part? About letting go of Danny? I need to, Grace. Your aunt is so right. It's a burden I shouldn't be bearing by myself. Ever since you came into my life I've been letting go of things."

"Right. Your house, your money, your sanity…"

He leaned his forehead against hers. "More like my troubles, my loneliness, my problems. You're always there for me, Grace. If I ask you, will you stay?"

"Of course." She could feel his hands grip her back. "So ask."

"You want it all out loud, don't you? Okay, here goes. Grace Mallory, I love you. Can we set a date, soon, for a real wedding?"

"Yes. As soon as we can get back to Redwing and arrange it all. Hal will have fun with this, won't he?"

"Definitely. I get the feeling he and Barb and Jo will all be busy for a while, plotting and planning for us. Think we could get Naomi to cater a reception?"

"Sure. We'll have to have cookies, the way you and the kids go through them."

"We'll have anything you want." He kissed her joyfully.

"Wow. There you go, giving things away again."

Carl picked her up and spun her around. Grace shrieked while he laughed. "You still don't get it, do you? Anything I've given away since I met you, I've gotten back tenfold." He set her down on the pavement. "Can I give away one more thing?"

"I guess. As long as it's yours to give."

"Great. I want to give you the store. Hire Jo to help you run it, or Janet, or both. But since you've come into my life, it's so plain that working in that store isn't where I'm meant to be. God has given me this talent for finding people, for helping them. I want to give that talent back to Him and see what we can do with it together." His eyes shone silver-gray.

"Carl, that's wonderful. Sure, I'll take the store. And you can find people. I wonder where it will lead."

"To good things, I'm sure. Knowing you has led to more good things than I could imagine. How can sharing the rest of my life with you lead to anything but more good things?"

Suddenly Four burst out of the woods, followed by two muddy kids and Jo. "Mama? Guess what? There's tadpoles in that creek back there. Do we have a jar in the truck? Can we bring some to Aunt Jo's?"

One of Four's muddy front paws was planted on Carl's jacket, the other on Grace's. Carl laughed at her reaction to the whole melee. "Tadpoles on top of everything else. How can this day possibly get any better?"

"It couldn't, Carl. Unless you kissed me again."

And he did, with the dog and kids and Jo looking on. And there in his arms, with mud on one cheek and wind pulling at her hair, Grace felt exultant, more blessed than ever before. "Thank you," she whispered.

To Carl or to God? Perhaps to both, because together they had given her more than she deserved, more than she had ever expected. These were truly gifts of grace. They filled her heart to overflowing.

*　*　*　*　*

Look for the brothers' reunion in
Mike Martin's love story, coming only
to Love Inspired in April 2000.

Dear Reader,

God is so good! I feel fortunate to have one of my great-aunts still living. Even though she is over ninety, and life has not always been easy, Esther begins most conversations and letters the way I have begun this letter to you. *God is so good.*

Sometimes when we get caught up in the daily tasks of living, it's easy to forget that. Why does it take so much to remind us, when the evidence is all around us? Grace's aunt in my book has a little bit of all of my grandfather's sisters in her character. They were women of great faith, and great humor as well. Their homes were always filled with laughter, prayer and the smell of good cooking, which is a trio that is hard to beat, in my mind.

God is so good. I hope the evidence of His goodness is everywhere in your life.

Blessings,

Lynn Bulock